BORDERLANDS

A DCI RYAN MYSTERY

LJ Ross

DCI RYAN MYSTERIES IN ORDER

1. Holy Island

2. Sycamore Gap

3. Heavenfield

4. Angel

5. High Force

6. Cragside

7. Dark Skies

8. Seven Bridges

9. The Hermitage

10. Longstone

11. The Infirmary (prequel)

12. The Moor

13. Penshaw

14. Borderlands

"The true soldier fights not because he hates what is in front of him, but because he loves what is behind him."

—G.K. Chesterton

PROLOGUE

Helmand Province, Afghanistan
August 2009

He wore flip-flops, the day Naseem died.

As the sun beat down upon the desert plains of Helmand Province at the end of the bloodiest summer of the Afghan War, he and his friend seated themselves on the banks of the Shamalan Canal and looked out across its muddy brown waters.

"One day, I'll show you my country," Naseem told him, in broken English. "When all of this is over, we'll take a boat and sail along the river. I'll show you what we're truly fighting for."

It was a pretty thought, and he allowed himself to imagine it. He saw a friendship that spanned continents and lasted a lifetime. Their wives would meet, their children would play, and they'd reminisce about their combat days over the thick black coffee Naseem liked to drink, and that he couldn't stand—especially in the stifling desert heat.

Pie in the sky, as his gran used to say.

"You should come over and see my country, too," he offered. "It's colder than here, but there are mountains and streams, and meadows of green grass…"

He trailed off, embarrassed to find a lump rising in his throat.

"It sounds beautiful," Naseem murmured, and then narrowed his eyes to look around what was left of his own war-torn land. "There were meadows here too."

They fell silent for a moment.

"We'd better be heading back. I'm on duty in an hour," he said, and reached for the rifle lying limply by his side.

The Black Watch—or, to give their infantry battalion its full title, the Black Watch, 3rd Battalion, Royal Regiment of Scotland—had been stationed on the canal since June of that year. It lay to the north of Lashkar Gar, the capital of Helmand Province, and had been wrestled from Taliban control during 'Operation Panther's Claw', one of the largest combined infantry and air assault operations undertaken by NATO forces. Coalition troops had succeeded in ousting the Taliban at three major crossing points on the Helmand River, hobbling their supply routes and forcing them further back into the dusty mountains.

While the fanfare resounded back in Whitehall, the Black Watch remained to guard the canal alongside their comrades in the Afghan National Army. Over the weeks that followed, the fighting became less fierce, daily attacks from the Taliban dwindled and, slowly, they began to relax.

Enough to wear flip-flops.

"We have time enough," Naseem replied. "Do you hear that?"

His body went on full alert, and he cocked his ear to listen for the sound of gunfire.

"I can't hear anything," he said, eventually.

"Exactly," Naseem replied, with a smile.

The two men stayed a while longer, telling tales about home while the insects buzzed in the undergrowth, until Naseem let out a small sound of surprise.

"He's back!"

A small, skinny-looking dog with the face of a wolf and a big, lolling tongue skipped its way through long grass further along the canal, stopping here and there to sniff the scorched earth.

Naseem rooted around his pockets until he found the small package of food he'd saved, and pushed to his feet, letting out a low whistle.

"He never comes when you make that noise," he said, brushing the dust from his shorts.

The animal was a stray and had never learned to come to a master's call, but he'd developed an understanding with the gentle Afghan captain who shared his food and ruffled his ears.

"He is proud," Naseem declared, and set off towards the reeds while his friend waited.

He cast his eyes over the canal, then back over his shoulder to the camp, which awaited their return. It had been a long summer, and an even longer tour, this time around. He'd seen too much destruction—too much for his soul to bear—and he was ready to go home.

One more month, he told himself. *Just one more month.*

In the early days, he'd believed in the cause; in fighting for Queen and Country. Now, he was tired, and bone-weary. He hated the sand and the heat, the blood and the toil. He longed for peace, that elusive thing they fought for, but feared would never come.

Suddenly irritable, he turned to leave.

"I'll see you later!" he called out.

Glancing back, he saw that Naseem was crouched a short distance from the reeds. His palm was outstretched, and he spoke softly to the dog, who raised his snout to the air and took a couple of tentative steps towards the food that was offered.

The soldier's breath caught in his throat.

As the dog emerged from the grass, he saw that a small improvised explosive device had been strapped to the underside of the animal's belly.

He watched in horror as it trotted over to his friend.

"Nas! Look out! Nas!"

He lunged forward, but an explosion of heat threw him back. He smelled his own burning flesh and began to roll, writhing around the dusty floor to extinguish the flames that licked his skin. There was a ringing in his ears; a deafening bell that drowned out all else, even his own howling cries of pain.

Across the sand, a small cloud of smoke rose up into the sunlit morning, taking his friend with it.

CHAPTER 1

Otterburn Army Training Ranges, Northumberland
Friday 16ᵗʰ August 2019

"CONTACT!"

When the Range Conducting Officer's voice broke into the quiet night air, Private Jess Stephenson threw herself to the valley floor with a thud, the force of the impact driving the air from her body in one hard *whoosh*. Unlike in a real combat scenario, no enemy shots were fired, but the section was supposed to role-play during the night-time live-fire tactical training exercise, because learning to react quickly could mean the difference between life and death on the battlefield.

Jess lay there in the bog, her body tensed and ready for action. Only when she heard the order did she haul herself up and continue onward, her boots squelching over the uneven ground. The darkness was almost overwhelming; the blackness so deep it seemed to close in and contract around her, as though it were a tangible, living thing. In the daylight, she knew there would be sweeping hills rising up on either side of the river, with the mighty Cheviot towering above them all. There would be forests in shades of green, and barren moors in a patchwork of brown and gold, littered with the carcases of abandoned tanks and artillery weapons, now rusted with age.

The Otterburn Ranges were situated in a remote corner of the world, covering ninety square miles of the Northumberland National Park, which was an area of outstanding natural beauty in the northernmost uplands where England met the border with Scotland. It was 'Reiver' territory; a wild frontier where battles had been waged hundreds of years before, and where men from both sides had slipped over the misty hills to pillage and rustle cattle from their neighbours by the light of the silvery moon. Now, the Ministry of Defence followed the tradition of warfare in that region by training its soldiers on its vast, open moorland.

But, without the moon to guide their way, the small section of the 1st Battalion, The Royal Welsh Fusiliers relied on their knowledge of the terrain and the night vision equipment attached to the front of their helmets, which was designed to track thermal heat. Somewhere out there was a moving target—a thermal contraption operated remotely by a Target Officer—and they were tasked with finding and neutralising it before sunrise.

Scanning either side of her, Jess counted two slow-moving figures to her left and another three to her right. She knew their names as well as she knew her own, but in this vast space of land and sky, they were little more than faceless, androgynous entities, just as she was.

She could feel herself beginning to tire, the muscles in her arms and legs burning with the effort of remaining upright, and she hiked the rifle up a little higher in defiance. She'd had enough well-meaning advice from family and friends about her decision to enlist—according to them, the army *wasn't suitable for a woman* and she would never have the physical strength or endurance required to be a soldier. No matter that she'd completed marathons and Ironman competitions, aced her basic training, and managed to outdo most of her male peers in the process.

Remembering that, she shifted the pack on her back and dug in her heels for the duration.

The section hiked over fences and through glens, along sodden burns and over rocky outcrops, clearing abandoned buildings as they went. It was slow, painstaking work, and her legs were trembling by the time the first, palest hint of dawn began to creep into the sky. It was little more than a lighter shade of navy blue, so it scarcely provided any respite and only served to remind them that they needed to find their target before the sun came up.

By mutual accord, their footsteps quickened, and they came to a flat, open range with a forest on one side. The section separated into a line and scanned left and right, tracking every knoll, every shadow and rock for a heat source.

Suddenly, there it was.

Through the night vision goggles she wore, Jess saw a flash of thermal imagery streak onto the horizon, about fifty yards up ahead.

"TARGET FRONT! CONTACT!" she shouted, and raised her weapon to fire.

Reverting to training, the outermost members of their section peeled away to move quickly around the side of their axis of advance, while she and the other central firers continued straight ahead.

Her finger curled around the trigger, and the first shot exploded into the night.

* * *

After the RCO called out, "STOP! STOP!", the small section locked their weapons and began the process of self-congratulatory back-slapping that was traditional at the end of a training exercise. Jess held back, finding herself preoccupied with a small, niggling doubt that wormed its way into her mind.

The target had gone down too quickly.

Normally, in exercises such as these, the RCO didn't press the electronic button for the target to fall until the section had expended most of their rounds trying to bring it down. But, in this case, the target had fallen almost immediately.

She slid her night vision goggles back on and peered through the gloom.

The target was still showing up as a heat source.

A slow, creeping feeling of dread began to spread through her body, and she shivered beneath the layers of protective armour she wore. Electronic thermal targets stopped emanating heat when they were switched off, as this one should have been.

Slowly, she began to walk towards the shadowy heap lying up ahead in the darkness, the toes of her boots scuffing the rocks at her feet. Behind the towering hills on the eastern edge of the valley, the sun rose higher in the sky, casting a thin, first light over the small group on the plains below.

"Hey! Where you goin'?" one of her section called out.

Jess ignored them and continued to walk towards the target, her heart hammering against the wall of her chest as she drew nearer.

As the first shaft of daylight burst down into the valley, she saw the target clearly.

"Oh—Oh, God, no—"

There came the sound of running footsteps and a moment later the RCO, a security officer and the medical officer puffed their way to where the section were standing in a rough circle.

"Packs and weapons on the ground, exactly where you're standing," one of them barked, while the other two ran ahead to where Jess stood frozen.

"Stephenson! Stand aside, and return to the section—that's an order."

Jess took a faltering step backwards while the medical officer went to work administering CPR, and the RCO made a hasty call back to camp, urgently requesting the emergency services.

But there would be nothing they could do, because it wasn't a mechanical target they'd fired upon; it was a woman, whose body now lay crumpled on the ground.

Jess looked down at the rifle she still held and let it slip from her nerveless fingers.

CHAPTER 2

When the call came from the Control Room shortly before six a.m., Detective Chief Inspector Maxwell Finlay-Ryan awoke instantly. There was no groggy fumbling as he reached for the phone on his bedside table, nor any bleary-eyed struggle as he processed the news that a life had been lost. There was only the same, aching sadness he felt every time; a sense of impotence at the waste, and the knowledge he could do nothing to change it. He could not bring back the dead.

But he could avenge them.

Ryan looked across at his wife, Anna. She was sleeping peacefully, but he knew that, somewhere under the same sky, another woman had not been so lucky.

He leaned across to brush his lips gently against hers, careful not to wake her, and then rolled out of bed to get dressed. Soon after, he was on the road, covering the short distance from his home in the picturesque village of Elsdon to the Otterburn Army Training Camp, six miles further west in the Northumbrian heartland.

* * *

An hour earlier, in the pretty market town of Wooler, Detective Sergeant Frank Phillips had thrust out an arm to quell the persistent ringing of his phone and banged it smartly against the metal edge of his new campervan.

"Yer *bugger!*"

"I beg your pardon?"

The question was delivered by his wife and boss in all things, including the police hierarchy. Having been rudely awakened, Detective Inspector Denise MacKenzie now regarded him from the other side of their bed with a cool, green-eyed stare.

"Sorry, love," he muttered, still rummaging for the phone. "I'm trying to find the blinkin'—"

A moment later, another irate female head appeared, hanging upside-down from the top bunk of the double bunk beds he'd fitted inside the vintage VW camper.

"What's all the racket?" Samantha asked, yawning hugely.

"Never you mind," Phillips grumbled. "I'm lookin' for—"

"Is this it?"

Samantha dangled the phone between her fingers, and he didn't bother to ask where she'd found it. The campervan might be small, but things had an uncanny knack of going missing, including most of the shortbread biscuits.

When he saw who the caller was, he threw back the covers and grabbed his coat, before taking it outside. Some things were not appropriate for young ears to hear, calls about murder being one of them.

* * *

The road was scenic and winding, taking Ryan along the underside of the Northumberland National Park and through the Cheviot Hills to the ancient village of Otterburn, thirty miles northwest of the Northumbria Police Headquarters in Newcastle upon Tyne, and a mere sixteen miles from the Scottish border. In days gone by, it had been the site of a major battle between the English and the Scots, but nowadays it serviced a large army community as well as tourists, hikers and wildlife enthusiasts who flocked to visit the area.

Ryan passed through the village and followed the road north until he came to the turning for the camp. There had been no other traffic on the road but, as he neared the military entrance, he found himself caught behind a slow-moving Volvo that he recognised on sight.

With a smile playing around the corners of his mouth, he punched a speed dial number on his hands-free system and waited for the driver up ahead to answer.

"Mornin'!"

Detective Sergeant Frank Phillips' unmistakably gruff voice boomed out of the car speakers, and Ryan hastily adjusted the volume control to avoid permanent damage to his ears.

"Are you nearly there?" he asked, wickedly.

"Aye, I'm on my way. Nearly at the entrance to the camp."

"Did you get stuck behind a tractor, or something?"

"For your information, I'm driving at the national speed limit," Phillips said, with dignity.

Ryan glanced at the speedometer on his own vehicle, which read less than thirty miles per hour, in a sixty zone.

He leaned on his horn, and gave a casual toot.

"Some joker behind is in a bleedin' hurry—" Phillips complained, and then glanced in his rear-view mirror.

Ryan waved at him.

"Oh, har bloody har," Phillips said, good-naturedly. "I s'pose you think you're funny?"

Ryan grinned.

"Shake a leg, Frank. This joker wants to get there sometime before nightfall."

* * *

They left any humour at the large security gates, which were manned by a pair of serious-looking armed guards. Once they'd been cleared for entry, the two detectives made their way along another winding road across undulating moorland until they reached Otterburn Training Camp. It was an extensive site, consisting of a collection of one and two-storey utilitarian buildings which had clearly been designed with functionality in mind, rather than style.

They proceeded directly to the guardroom, where they were met by a small welcoming party.

"I'm Detective Chief Inspector Ryan, and this is my sergeant, Frank Phillips. We're from Northumbria CID," he said, drawing out his warrant card for inspection.

A clean-cut, uniformed man of around fifty stepped forward and extended his hand, which Ryan took.

"Thank you for coming so quickly," he said, in a soft Scottish burr that was common in the borders. "I'm 2nd Lieutenant Pat Dalgliesh, and this is Corporal Amanda Huxley. I was the Range Conducting Officer for last night's live-fire tactical exercise and Corporal Huxley was one of our safety supervisors."

Ryan nodded politely.

"Thank you for meeting us," he said. "What steps have been taken, so far?"

Dalgliesh indicated that they should walk and talk, and began to lead them from the guardroom towards a battered-looking army jeep parked in the forecourt nearby.

"At around oh-five-twenty hours, a section from the Royal Welsh came across what they believed to be a thermal target, and opened fire," he said.

"The point of the exercise was to locate and neutralise two moving thermal targets, simulated at a running speed," Huxley put in. "Without any natural light source, the section relied on their night vision equipment which picks up thermal energy. They found the first target as planned, and then proceeded to look for the second. The locale was very dark and otherwise deserted. At that hour, I don't think anybody could have expected to find a civilian on the ranges. It's a terrible tragedy."

Ryan made no comment, but thought privately that it seemed the army had already begun to close ranks to protect its own.

"Both myself and Corporal Huxley attended the scene immediately and called a stop to the exercise when we became aware of the false target," Dalgliesh said, after he'd settled himself behind the wheel. "We called in the medical officer, who was with us, and then radioed back to camp, who called the emergency services immediately. We moved the casualty via stretcher around half a mile further east, to be nearer the access road, and I believe the paramedics arrived shortly before six."

Neither Ryan nor Phillips queried the time it had taken the ambulance service to arrive on-scene. The Northumberland National Park was a vast area of land, much of which was largely inaccessible other than on foot or with an all-terrain vehicle. He also happened to know that the nearest air ambulance helicopter was based in Hull, and wouldn't have arrived any sooner—even if it had been authorised for night service in the region.

Dalgliesh sighed, and started up the engine.

"Our soldiers are trained to act quickly, and according to instructions. As Corporal Huxley says, it's extremely regrettable, but that's why the controlled access area is clearly marked with red 'danger' flags and signage to the public not to enter."

"Where is the victim now?" Ryan asked, and the other two exchanged an uncomfortable glance at his descriptor.

"The scene of the incident is approximately twelve miles north of here, near Witch Crags, which is roughly in the middle of the controlled access zone," Dalgliesh said, and steered the car along one of a network of smaller roads giving access to the more remote parts of the training ranges. "Having been pronounced dead at the scene, the casualty was transported by ambulance to the larger mortuary in Newcastle."

Ryan nodded, and made a note to contact the police pathologist.

"What about the trainees?" Phillips asked.

"When we stopped the exercise, they were instructed to remove their packs and to set down their rifles," Huxley replied, looking over her shoulder from the front passenger seat. "It's protocol whenever there's an incident like this, to mark the position of firers on the range."

"Makes sense," Phillips said. "We'll need to confiscate the gear and the weapons, for ballistics."

She nodded.

"We've got an investigator on the way from Defence AIB," she said, referring to the Accident Investigation Branch responsible for conducting independent inquiries into service-related fatalities and other major incidents. "They should be here within the hour. They'll be able to unload and hand over the weapons for testing."

The Defence Accident Investigation Branch fell under the remit of the Defence Safety Authority, which in turn fell under the authority of the Ministry of Defence. Its investigators were supposed to defer to the primacy of the regional police Major Crimes Unit, but in Ryan and Phillips' limited experience of army-civilian fatalities, this wasn't always the case.

"Has the forensics team arrived?"

Dalgliesh shook his head and made a sharp right turn along another barren road, where the wind blew in across the fields and buffeted the sides of the car as it made its lonely way over the moorland.

"We've given directions for the CSIs to use the army access roads, and I've stationed soldiers at checkpoints to guide them in from the main road at Harbottle when they arrive," he explained. "In the meantime, we transported the section back to base as they were beginning to display signs of shock. Their clothing has been confiscated and held in plastic bags, and they've been given a warm meal alongside some debriefing."

Quick work, Ryan thought, and ample opportunity for members of the training section to confer, as well as for commanding officers to 'debrief' along party lines, if they wished to.

Perhaps he was growing cynical, in his old age.

Time would tell.

CHAPTER 3

An hour before dawn, Imam Aayan Abdullah had left the modest terraced house he owned in an area of Newcastle upon Tyne known as 'Arthur's Hill' and made his way towards the Central Mosque. It lay to the west of the city centre, overlooking rows of residential houses and shops running all the way down to the banks of the River Tyne, in a vibrant, multi-cultural area where people of all skins and faiths flocked to enjoy the best sugary *dodol* that side of the Indian sub-continent.

The sky was still a deep, navy blue speckled with stars as he made his way through the quiet streets, but he knew that, before dawn, the streets would bustle as men—and women—of his faith flocked to the mosque to say their Fajr Prayer, the first of five daily prayers in the Muslim faith. The Imam was proud of the community he served; of the way it pulled together in times of hardship to offer free food and clothing to the needy, and of its outreach programme that aimed to break down barriers and show people that the true followers of Islam practised peace and submission, not hatred.

He allowed himself to hope that, in a few more years, he'd be able to walk down the street without seeing fear and mistrust in the eyes of his neighbours. His mind was pleasantly occupied with these optimistic thoughts, when he heard what sounded like an enormous firework exploding somewhere nearby.

With a sense of foreboding, he hurried along the main road to where a small crowd of people had gathered.

And then, he saw what they saw.

The mosque they'd worked and saved so hard to build was burning, orange flames crawling over its carved wooden doors like serpents. A large black symbol depicting three interlocking triangles had been spray-painted on its white walls, alongside the message, 'MUSLIMS GO HOME'.

In the distance, Abdullah heard the sound of sirens approaching, and knew that one of his brothers or sisters must have called for help. Around him, the community stood solemnly and looked to him for guidance, so he set aside his personal sadness and drew on his strength to counsel forgiveness and love.

Behind the burning building, the dawn began to rise, and his heart was heavy as he prepared to tell those who shared his faith to go back to their homes, and pray there instead.

But, before he could speak, he felt a hand on his shoulder.

"Come and use our hall," the priest offered, and nodded in the direction of a small, Christian community hall tucked behind the main road. "It might be a squeeze to get everyone in, but you're welcome."

The Imam held the man's hand in both of his own.

"*Jazak Allahu Khayran*," he murmured. "Thank you, my friend."

* * *

Detective Constable Jack Lowerson was otherwise *very* pleasantly occupied when the call came from the Control Room to attend the scene at Newcastle Central Mosque and, for the first time in his career, he found himself torn between a desire to serve and an even greater desire to stay exactly where he was, possibly for the rest of his life.

"Who was that?" a sleepy voice asked, and he turned to smile into the eyes of his newly-promoted colleague and—he dared to say—*girlfriend*, Detective Constable Melanie Yates.

"Control," he replied, while his eyes roamed over her flushed skin and spiky cap of blonde hair. "There's been a hate attack on the

Central Mosque. Ryan's already attending an incident up in Otterburn with Phillips, so this one's ours."

Melanie's eyes clouded with sadness, and she sat up straighter in bed.

"What kind of attack?" she asked.

"Arson," he replied. "The fire's still raging now."

"That's dreadful," she said, softly. "Was anybody hurt?"

"Not that they know of," Lowerson murmured, and curved an arm around her shoulder when she laid her head against his chest. "That makes two attacks on non-Christian places of worship, in as many weeks."

She nodded, and the top of her hair brushed the underside of his chin.

"Arson in both cases, too. D'you think they're connected?"

"There's only one way to find out," he said, and threw back the covers so the cool morning air hit them both in a rush.

"Time to go to work," he declared.

But, before he padded towards the bathroom, she tugged him back to her and bestowed a slow, thorough kiss.

"To be continued," she murmured.

It took his brain less than a second to reject that option, and her eyes widened when he plucked her off the bed and up into his arms.

"On second thought, it'll be much quicker if we shower together, don't you think?"

"Very sensible," she agreed, and broke into a wide smile.

CHAPTER 4

The sky was a bright, bold blue by the time the Jeep reached a small mass of water known as 'Linshiels Lake', on the eastern edge of the Controlled Area and not far from the village of Harbottle. A number of other army vehicles were parked nearby, as well as a plain, unmarked van they knew belonged to Tom Faulkner, the senior CSI attached to Northumbria CID.

"We have to go on foot from here, but it's not far to walk," Dalgliesh said, and slammed out of the vehicle. "All of this area falls within the controlled zone, but the lake is protected from fire since there's a dam attached to it. The training plan for last night's exercise took the section through the middle—between the lake and Witch Crags, a couple of miles further west. That's the direction we go from here."

At the thought of having to walk for at least a mile, Phillips looked down at his comfortably worn-in hiking boots and then made a surreptitious inspection of Ryan's feet, half expecting to find them clad in a pair of fancy suede shoes. Instead, he was surprised to see a pair of scuffed, top-of-the-range boots in their place.

Noticing the direction of his gaze, Ryan's lips twitched.

"The last time we were called out to the middle of nowhere, I seem to recall I almost fell arse-first over Hadrian's Wall," he explained. "I learned my lesson."

"Glad to know some of my good sense is rubbing off," Phillips said. "We'll move on to your southern mispronunciation of the word 'scone', next."

Ryan snorted, and looked out across the wide, open space.

There was both beauty and isolation in that part of the country, which had allowed rare species of birds and mammals to flourish without man's interference—and the hills and crags, burns and lakes provided endless opportunities for quiet contemplation for those who sought it. However, it was also a detective's nightmare; an enormous mass of gullies and caves, of abandoned buildings and woodland where dark deeds could and probably *did* happen.

"It's a logistical nightmare," Ryan murmured, as they waited for Dalgliesh and Huxley to finish having a word with one of the sentry officers standing guard over the vehicles parked at the side of the road.

Phillips nodded, and screwed up his face against the sun as he looked out across miles of untamed wilderness.

"Aye, and I can't help wondering what somebody was doing all the way out here, at that hour of the morning," he said. "Anybody planning to come out here would know which areas to avoid, and we've seen how hard it is to wind up in this neck of the woods purely by accident."

Ryan agreed.

"It's too far from any campsite or tourist destination to be accidental," he said. "Therefore, we have to assume the visit to the Controlled Area was planned, or for some other reason, as yet unknown."

"*Suspicious*, you mean," Phillips put in, with his usual forthrightness.

Ryan smiled, and nodded.

"You know what struck me, Frank? From the outset, both officers have been very keen to tell us how accidental and tragic the whole thing is. That may still be true, but they also told us the section was given orders to neutralise a moving thermal target, simulated to run. You know what that means?"

Phillips nodded grimly.

"It means the lass was running, when she was hit."

"Exactly," Ryan murmured. "And we need to find out what she was running from, or to."

There was a short, meaningful pause, and then Phillips heaved a long sigh.

"Well, there go my plans for a peaceful few days at the holiday camp," he said.

Ryan gave him a bolstering slap on the back, and they began to follow the two army officers, who set a brisk pace across the moorland.

"Chin up, Frank. You'll be back with Sam and Denise toasting marshmallows before you know it."

* * *

It may not have been toasted marshmallows, but Phillips would have shed a manly tear if he'd known that, at the very moment his boot connected with a large pile of sheep dung, Denise and their foster daughter were tucking into a couple of bacon stotties, fresh out of the oven from a mobile van that passed through Wooler every morning.

"I think I like the ones from *The Pie Van* best," Samantha declared, between bites of bacon smeared in ketchup. "I'm particular about my bacon sandwiches."

"You're getting as bad as Frank," MacKenzie chuckled, as they made their way towards the swimming pool. "It's a shame he's still on duty, but at least we can spend a bit of time together."

Samantha felt a warm glow spread through her belly. Never, in all her life, had anybody told her they were happy to be spending time with her, until now.

"Are you looking forward to going back to school?" MacKenzie asked.

There hadn't been much in the way of a regular routine for Sam, and the process of starting school and making new friends had been a challenge, to begin with. But, soon enough, she'd made a nice group of friends and they'd been relegated to little more than glorified taxi drivers to facilitate the ten-year-old's newfound social life during the long summer holidays.

"Yeah, it'll be nice to go back, but I'm sick of talking about *boys*."

MacKenzie almost choked on her bacon sandwich.

"Right," she said, dumbly. "There's been a lot of talk about boys, has there?"

Samantha nodded.

"There's a disco on the first Friday back at school, and everybody thinks Jamie Webb is going to ask me to dance with him, but I said Jamie Webb is too young for me—"

"Aren't you the same age?" MacKenzie enquired, mildly.

"Well, *yes*, but he's sooo immature. I mean, he still collects Pokémon cards," Samantha said, and pulled an expressive face. "Anyway, I definitely won't be dancing with him. Unless he swaps his Pikachu card with me," she added, as an afterthought.

"But, I thought you said—"

"I'm keeping my options open," the girl said, wisely.

MacKenzie shook her head in bemusement, wondering if there was a reference manual for moments such as these. As a woman in her mid-forties, while Frank was more than a decade older, the pair of them had practically ruled out the possibility of having children of their own. That was the way of it, sometimes; she'd spent the first twenty years of her adult life searching, but only found the person to share her life with after most women had already married and had their babies. It had never really bothered her, and they'd certainly been very happy on their own, but deciding to take Samantha into their hearts and hearth had been a revelation. All the same, parenting was no easy task, as she was learning every day.

Suddenly, she felt a twinge run through her bad leg.

A couple of years before, she had been the hostage of a violent killer, and escape had not come without a cost. The blade of his knife had torn ligaments and nerves, causing her leg to cramp and seize, and for a phantom pain to follow her throughout the day. She knew that some of it was psychosomatic; a kind of echo of the trauma and fear she'd once suffered. But, no matter how much she attended physiotherapy classes or counselling courses, no matter how much she forced herself to keep going, the pain remained real and could sometimes take her by surprise.

"Are you okay?" Samantha asked, having watched the blood drain from MacKenzie's face.

"I'll be fine," she managed, clasping a hand to her leg. "I just—I just need to sit down."

As she staggered towards one of the nearby benches, she found herself wondering whether she would ever be able to escape the long shadow the *Hacker* still cast upon their lives.

The child was sensitive, and intelligent; Samantha sat beside the woman she was coming to think of as 'mother' and didn't ask the burning question she longed to ask: how Denise had hurt herself. Instead, she simply reached across to take her hand and held it tightly in her own small fingers.

Denise looked down at their joined hands, and then into the small, freckled face, and smiled.

CHAPTER 5

B y the time they reached the site of the incident, Phillips was puffing hard after covering the ground in what he would have described as indecent haste. To his chagrin, the mile-long hike didn't seem to have posed too much of a challenge to the other three, and he told himself it was high time he went on a diet.

"There's Faulkner," Ryan said, and raised an arm to hail the Senior CSI, who had arrived shortly before them with two members of his small crew. They were hard to miss, dressed as they were in white polypropylene coveralls which stood out amid the brownish-green landscape of the valley.

As they'd walked, flat plains had given way to the sharp rise and fall of the lower Cheviot Hills, dipping towards a wide valley where a series of small burns flowed. In the middle of it all, a small huddle of men and women had gathered, partly camouflaged by the khaki green of their uniforms.

Ryan paused to take a sweeping look around the vicinity, raising a hand to shield his eyes from the glare of the sun. From his position on higher ground, the army and police personnel on the valley bed seemed to move like ants; their bodies seemingly insignificant in the wide, open space of land and sky. If their presence was hard to spot in broad daylight, he could only imagine the challenge in pitch darkness.

It sent an odd shudder up his spine, and the tiny hairs on the back of his neck prickled.

"Which way was she running?" Ryan asked, of the two army officers.

"West to east," Huxley replied, after a small pause. "From the underside of Witch Crags, over there, in this direction."

She pointed to illustrate the direction of travel.

"The section was headed north," she continued, and traced another line in the air. "The real target is another half-mile in that direction."

"So, you knew straight away, they'd made a mistake," Phillips put in.

Dalgliesh nodded.

"We shouted the command to 'STOP' but, as I said earlier, they responded quickly to a perceived target. There were six firers on the ground, and we believe all of them expended ammunition."

Ryan's face became shuttered as he thought of what might be left of the poor soul who was now lost to the world. Until he knew the full circumstances, he would not pronounce judgment; it was the job of a soldier to defend their country, and that required the proper training. But it was *his* job to investigate the unlawful taking of a life, and he knew from hard-earned experience that didn't require a full magazine of ammunition.

It only required a single bullet.

* * *

As they reached the small group of soldiers and civilians, a tall, broad-shouldered man of around fifty spotted their arrival and peeled away from the rest. As he approached, both Dalgliesh and Huxley came to attention.

"At ease," he said, in well-rounded tones. "You must be from the police."

"Y' sir. This is DCI Ryan and Sergeant Phillips, from Northumbria CID," Dalgliesh said. "This is our Commanding Officer, Lieutenant Colonel Theodore Robson."

He nodded to them both, and exchanged a firm handshake.

"Sad business," he said, without preamble. "Your forensics team have just arrived, but we took some pictures prior to that, which we're happy to make available."

"Thank you," Ryan said, and looked across to the other members of the assembled crowd. "Perhaps you could introduce us to any other witnesses who were present at the time of the incident, last night? Through the course of the day, we'd like to interview all members of the section as well as any other army personnel who played a part in the exercise."

"Of course," Robson said. "I'll make sure they're made available to you. It would be in all our interests to complete the necessary formalities before close of business tomorrow, when the company is due to move out."

Ryan raised a single eyebrow, and gave a slight shake of his head.

"I'm sorry, I can't give you any assurance that our preliminary investigation will be finished by tomorrow evening. Until such time as our interviews and enquiries are complete, it would be helpful for the platoon to remain encamped at Otterburn."

If Ryan had expected some resistance, he was pleasantly surprised.

"Naturally, I understand. I'll make all necessary arrangements," Robson said, without hesitation. "If there's anything else I can do to assist, you have only to ask."

Ryan thanked him.

"I'll introduce you to the other key members of last night's exercise," Robson continued, signalling the remaining three uniformed officers to join them. "Here, we have my second-in-command, Major Owen Jones, whose job it is to plan and maintain an accurate record of training undertaken by all our soldiers; Gwen Davies, Company Sergeant Major for the 1st Royal Welsh; and Corporal Rhys Evans, who was our Target Officer during last night's training. Our Medical

Officer is Major Rupert Sanderson, who returned to base earlier this morning to oversee the troops' debriefing."

Ryan nodded, and turned to his sergeant.

"Frank, if you wouldn't mind taking down initial statements from these officers, I'll have a word with Faulkner," he said, and then turned back to the CO. "We appreciate your cooperation."

With that, he turned and strode purposefully across the moor.

* * *

Back at camp, Private Jessica Stephenson couldn't stop the tremor in her hands.

Her eyes darted around the room where she'd been asked to wait, and she wondered whether the other members of her section had also been singled out and were pacing the floor of their own holding cell.

For that's what it was; she was under no illusions about that.

They'd been stripped of their weapons and clothing and, after a chat with the Medical Officer about actions in the 'line of duty', had been separated pending police investigation.

And, in the silent room, left with only her own thoughts for company, her mind began to unravel. *Had she killed that woman?*

She sank onto the edge of a single camp bed and held her head in her hands, trying to remember every detail of what had happened.

It had been dark—so dark—and she'd struggled to see clearly. Even now, her eyes felt teary and blurred from the strain, and her body cried out for sleep.

But she would not sleep.

She couldn't.

Jess held her hands out in front of her and stared at them; at the skin, at the shadows of veins and capillaries throbbing beneath, and thought of the other woman's hands as they'd lain motionless in the dirt.

With a sob, she curled up onto the bed and tucked her knees against her chest.

The trembling continued.

CHAPTER 6

First responders from the local police station had set up a cordon of sorts, consisting of a line spray-painted on the ground to prevent further contamination of the incident site. Beyond it, Faulkner's team of CSIs were busy erecting a small forensics tent around a small patch of earth where the fatality occurred, and the man himself was taking a series of photographs of the wider scene as well as more detailed shots of the valley floor, using a high-spec camera.

Ryan stopped at the painted line and entered his name in the logbook, which was being kept by one of the local constables and of which he approved. It didn't matter what the terrain; procedures were in place for good reason.

"Tom!"

Faulkner turned at the sound of his name and raised a hand in greeting, then beckoned Ryan forward. The latter paused to cover his shoes in blue plastic coverings, then stepped over the line and into the crime scene.

"Good to see you, Ryan," the CSI said, and pushed up the mask he wore to reveal an average, pale-skinned face badly in need of a shave. "Early start, today."

"No rest for the wicked," Ryan shrugged. "What've we got here?"

"A forensic nightmare," he replied, bluntly. "Even if we weren't outside and open to the elements, there must have been ten or more people trampling around the site here before we were able to secure it. I'd say we'll probably be here for the rest of the day."

"Understood." There was little point in wishing it were otherwise; Ryan knew the kind of careful, intricate work required of a forensic team and it was in nobody's interests for that work to be rushed.

"We'll start with the spot where the victim died, and move out in expanding circles," Faulkner continued. "I've taken some shots of the area, and of the spatter pattern, which seems to be in line with what you'd expect."

Ryan's eyes strayed to the ground, which was now partially concealed by the flapping tent, and saw an angry reddish-brown stain.

"Anything else of note?"

Faulkner sighed, and scratched the top of his head with a gloved hand.

"The CO said the woman would have been running in this direction," he said, indicating a westerly motion. "If that's the case, I'm going to focus on the area she was most likely to have crossed, and see if it turns up any other useful clues. Do we know who she was?"

"She hasn't been identified," Ryan murmured. "No personal effects on her, no purse or handbag, but she could already be in the system as a Missing Person."

Faulkner nodded, sadly.

"Have you considered—?"

"That she didn't run out into the line of fire by accident? Yes, it's a possibility," Ryan said, in a low voice. "We won't know the likely answer until we find out who she was, and what her life was like; whether she posed a risk to herself."

Faulkner made a rumbling noise of sympathy.

"I feel sorry for whoever fired the fatal shot," he said. "They were following their training, but it won't feel that way, just now."

Ryan stuck his hands in his pockets and looked out across the ranges, then back to where Phillips was making his way around the small group of army officers, exercising his inimitable charm to great effect.

"I feel sorrier for the victim," he was bound to say. "But I agree with you. In their marksmanship training, the targets are made to look human, so trainees won't be afraid to pull the trigger when they need to, on the battlefield. It's hard to blame a soldier for following orders, to the letter."

He paused before continuing.

"All the same, this isn't a battlefield—and that woman wasn't a target."

* * *

Private Jess Stephenson's eyes flew open at the sound of a brief knock on the door, and she hurriedly stood to attention, rubbing sleep from her eyes. She must have nodded off at some point, but it had been a fitful sleep, filled with dark, nightmarish shapes that clawed at her skin.

She looked down at her hands, then clasped them behind her back as the door opened.

Sergeant Major Gwen Davies entered with two other men in tow, neither of whom she recognised. One was somewhere in his late thirties; tall, dark, and movie-star handsome, if she'd been thinking clearly enough to notice. The other was in his mid-fifties, with a shorter, stockier build and button-brown eyes that were presently full of compassion.

"At ease, Private," Davies said. "Stephenson, this is DCI Ryan and DS Phillips, from Northumbria CID. They're here to take a statement from you, as part of their investigation."

Jess nodded, feeling a bit light-headed.

"Would it be possible to get a glass of orange juice, or something sugary, in here?" the taller one asked, and she sent him a grateful look.

The Sergeant Major nodded and excused herself.

"Private Stephenson—do you mind if we call you Jessica?"

"I prefer Jess," she said quietly.

"Thank you." Ryan indicated that she should sit. "We're here to ask you some questions about what happened, if you're feeling up to it?"

"I'll do my best."

"It's all normal routine," Phillips reassured her. "We'll be asking the same of everyone who was on the exercise, last night."

She swallowed.

"Do I—do I need a lawyer, or anything like that?"

"We'll be asking you these questions under caution, so you're entitled to a lawyer if you'd like one," Ryan said, evenly. "We can wait, if you'd like to make a call?"

She searched their faces, and then shook her head.

"No, it's alright. I'll answer whatever I can."

Ryan smiled, and pulled out one of two spindly plastic chairs arranged around a small table in the corner of the room. Then, he recited the standard caution.

"Do you understand those rights and responsibilities?" he asked.

She nodded, and was grateful when the door opened again to admit the Sergeant Major, who brought a tall glass of orange juice with her.

Jess drank it in four large gulps, and then stared down at the glass she held in her hands.

When she looked up, her eyes were twin pools of misery.

"It was me," she whispered. "I was the one who killed her."

CHAPTER 7

The dog was following him, again.

From his perch beneath the concrete flyover, the soldier watched a small, scruffy-looking dog skip towards him with the same, dopey-eyed grin on its face he'd seen somewhere before, on the banks of the Shamalan Canal.

"Bugger off!" he slurred, and hurled an empty can of beer in its direction.

The dog wavered, and then plonked its bum a safe distance away, where it continued to stare at him with big, baleful eyes.

"Why don't you leave me alone?" he asked, speaking half to himself. "I don't *like* you. I don't *want* you, alright?"

The dog's tail began to wag, and he made a sound that was somewhere between a sob and a laugh. Overhead, early morning traffic whizzed around the roundabout and over the Tyne Bridge, or into the centre of Newcastle, as people went about their daily grind.

He remembered doing that, once.

After the army, he'd tried becoming a civilian. What other choice had they given him? He couldn't stay in the Watch, not if he couldn't fire a gun or follow a basic command anymore.

And so, he'd come home.

They told him there were groups for men like him; places he could go, people he could talk to.

He'd joined the waiting list for some of them.

And waited.

And waited.

In the meantime, he'd drank on Friday and Saturday nights with his old civvie friends, who told him stories about being estate agents and mortgage brokers. He'd watched them flirt with women in bars, while he'd fought rising panic and claustrophobia, and the crippling knowledge that he no longer looked like everybody else.

Until, one day, they stopped asking him to join them, and he'd taken to drinking on his own.

He'd tried to get a job, but there were few available for men like him. Maybe, if he'd finished his training, or if he had a brother who could put in a good word…but there was nobody. He'd gone through the care system before enlisting, and he wouldn't know his family if they passed him on the street.

Eventually, he'd picked up a few hours at a factory, making exhausts for the latest motors coming off the production line. It had been alright at first, but then they'd moved him to another section, where they said they'd train him to weld.

Sparks everywhere, and the hissing sound of flame hitting metal.

Like the fire that had melted his skin, and reduced Naseem to ash.

They'd found him huddled in the corner, with his hands over his ears.

They said there were people he could talk to, about things like that. Doctors, and psychologists, or something.

And then, they'd let him go.

The soldier looked over at the dog, but found him gone, too.

* * *

When Lowerson and Yates arrived at the Central Mosque, they found two fire engines in attendance, having spent over an hour working to extinguish the blaze. Exterior walls that had once been white were now a charred grey, and the interior was little more than a damp, hollowed-out shell. Local police had set up a safety cordon to keep back a crowd of locals, who spilled out onto the main road and blocked early-morning commuter traffic as people made their way into the city centre.

They found a parking space several streets away, and when Lowerson and Yates returned they sought out the First Responding Officer.

"PC Zadir? DC Lowerson and DC Yates, from CID."

They flashed their warrant cards and signed the logbook before slipping beneath the plastic cordon.

"What happened here?" Lowerson asked of the young police constable.

"Ah, well sir, several calls came through to the Control Room at around five-thirty this morning reporting a fire," Zadir began. "I was dispatched along with PC Sheldon to the scene, as there was a strong suspicion of arson. The Fire Service arrived a few minutes before us and were already in the process of fighting the blaze, so we focused our efforts on keeping the crowds under control and setting up a safety cordon. We sought and received authority to set up a roadblock, and traffic is now being diverted into town, sir."

"Good work," Yates murmured, and the younger man nodded his thanks.

"We took preliminary statements from the imam and several other eyewitnesses, who claim they heard a loud, popping explosion before the fire broke out."

"Has the Fire Investigator arrived, yet?" Yates asked.

Zadir turned and pointed to a woman standing a short distance away, chatting to one of the firemen.

"They need to make sure the building's safe to enter, before she can go inside," he explained.

"Alright. What about the witnesses—were there any reports of persons fleeing the scene, or acting suspiciously?" Lowerson asked.

But Zadir shook his head.

"None, sir. Most people were still in their homes, until the sound of the explosion."

Lowerson nodded, and cast his gaze around the street until he spotted a man dressed in traditional loose robes, speaking to a small group of locals.

"Is that the imam?"

Zadir nodded.

"There's something else, sir," he said, and fished out his smartphone to bring up a series of photographs. "When we arrived, we could see a message and some kind of symbol had been graffitied onto the wall, so I took some pictures in case it was destroyed in the fire."

He handed over the phone, and the two detectives put their heads together to scroll through the images. When they came to the first picture of three interlocking triangles, they paused and exchanged a worried glance.

It was the same symbol they'd seen a week before, spray-painted in blood red onto the side of a synagogue on the other side of the river, in Gateshead.

"It wasn't isolated," she murmured.

"We've got a terror group on our hands," Lowerson agreed, and felt his heart sink.

He had been born in the north of England and was proud to call it home; he was proud of its landscape, its culture and the warmth of its people, whose generosity of spirit was the stuff of legend.

But now, as he thought of his kinfolk banding together to inflict fear and hatred upon those who were different from themselves...

Now, he felt ashamed.

CHAPTER 8

After interviewing each of the six firers who participated in the live-fire training exercise the previous day, Ryan and Phillips emerged back into the early afternoon sunshine and stood quietly for a moment, watching a flock of birds rise up into the sky.

"We won't know until the ballistics report comes back whether Jess Stephenson was the one to fire the fatal shot," Ryan said, as they watched a small section of troops line up outside their barracks on the far side of the base. "Clearly, she feels responsible, but a couple of the others felt equally culpable."

"It could have been any one of them," Phillips agreed. "Fact is, it was an easy mistake to make, in the circumstances—not that I expect the victim's family to see things that way."

"Where do we draw the line, Frank?" Ryan wondered aloud. "I know what the law says about lawful and unlawful killing but, I'm asking you—where do we draw the moral line?"

Phillips let out a long sigh and ran a hand over the stubble on his jaw. Ryan's world was so clearly drawn in shades of black and white, it was hard for him to comprehend the many shades of grey in between. That wasn't to say he was naïve, nor that he hadn't experienced many of them first-hand, but he lived by a strict moral compass that seldom wavered. To him, killing was always killing, no matter the circumstances.

His conviction was the only thing that had stopped Ryan from taking a life himself, not so very long ago, and so he chose his words with care.

"The thing is, lad, being a soldier isn't all that different from being a doctor, or a nurse...even a teacher. You've got the capacity to kill people in any of those professions, and I don't just mean physically. You can kill somebody's dream with a few harsh words, or their spirit, just as easily as you can stop their heart from beating. At least, when you're fighting for Queen and Country, you're fighting for something bigger than yourself. You're fighting for a way of life."

Further discussion was forestalled by the arrival of 2nd Lieutenant Dalgliesh, who brought with him a new visitor.

"DCI Ryan, DS Phillips, this is Major Alice Malloy, who's a senior investigator from the Defence AIB."

Both men received a firm, no-nonsense handshake.

"I'm sorry I was delayed," she said. "Shall we find a meeting space, and discuss the progress that's been made so far?"

She didn't wait for an answer but swept past them both and made directly for the Officers' Mess, leaving them little option but to follow.

* * *

"I've facilitated the turnover of weapons to your forensic team," Major Malloy began, once they were seated in a quiet corner of the mess. It was a serviceable room, with taupe-coloured walls and a lingering scent of shepherd's pie, which bore a strong resemblance to the staff canteen back at Police Headquarters.

"Thank you," Ryan said, politely. "The sooner we can get things moving along with ballistics, the better."

Malloy nodded, and linked her fingers on the tabletop.

"It can sometimes be tricky, managing the relationship between an army investigator, and a civilian police force—" she began.

"Oh, I'm sure we'll get along just fine," Ryan said, and gave her one of his best smiles. "Provided we remember that, legally, Northumbria CID has primacy over this investigation."

Malloy pursed her lips, and tried another approach.

"My role is to conduct an independent investigation into the incident, so that the panel can assess whether there are any lessons to be learned from the army's handling of the live-fire exercise. I have no desire to impede the progress of your own investigation, chief inspector, but I'm sure you can appreciate the value in finding out if there are ways to prevent a similar occurrence, in future."

Ryan nodded.

"I can," he said. "So, let's negotiate terms, Major Malloy."

He linked his own hands on the tabletop, and smiled.

"Here's the deal: we'll share pertinent details of our investigation with you, including access to interviews and external reports, if you'll afford us the same courtesy. I don't want this turning into a closed shop, with interviews being conducted outside of the main investigation. Is that agreed?"

Malloy knew a good deal when she heard it.

"Agreed," she said, and then flipped open a notepad. "I understand you've already interviewed the firers from last night's training exercise. Do you mind sharing copies of those interviews?"

"I'll have them typed and sent to you by the end of the day," Ryan said. "But I can tell you their stories are almost identical. Four out of six members of the section spotted a fast-moving thermal target crossing their line of sight, at around quarter past five, this morning. Of those four, Private Jess Stephenson was the one to sound the alarm, following which they engaged the 'target' and opened fire."

Malloy made swift notes on her pad, and then looked up.

"Do we know who was the first to open fire?"

"Stephenson is convinced she was the one to fire the first shot," Phillips put in, returning to the table with three mugs of steaming tea. "A couple of the others seem to think it was them. We haven't interviewed any of the officers involved in the tactical exercise, yet."

Malloy nodded, and tapped her pen.

"What do we know about the deceased?"

"Almost nothing," Ryan said. "I made a call to the pathologist's office earlier this morning, but it was too soon for him to tell us anything useful. We'll stop by the hospital later this evening or tomorrow morning, and see if anything's changed. As it stands, we've found nothing to identify the victim; there were no personal items found on or near her body. The CSIs have been conducting a detailed search of the vicinity since early this morning, and have found no personal items discarded anywhere nearby."

"Missing Persons?" Malloy queried.

"That was one thing the pathologist was able to tell us," Ryan said, softly. "The victim suffered considerable trauma to her face, such that it may prove difficult to search for a match on the database using photographs alone."

"God rest her soul," Malloy whispered, and then cleared her throat. "What the DAIB needs to know is whether the signage was ineffective in providing a warning to civilians living or travelling in the area. They'll want to know if there's more that could have been done."

Ryan and Phillips exchanged an eloquent look.

"Unless further evidence comes to light, we're giving serious consideration to the possibility this might have been a case of planned suicide," Ryan explained. "The army publishes a comprehensive schedule of its planned training exercises, sometimes months in advance, including locations in order to help civilians to avoid those areas in particular. It wouldn't be impossible for somebody to use that information improperly, and it seems significant that the victim had no rucksack or other possessions with her when she died."

Malloy heaved a gusty sigh.

"If that turns out to be the case, it's a hell of a burden for a young soldier to carry," she said quietly. "They're trained to repel enemies and protect their country with force, if necessary—not to perform assisted suicides."

Ryan thought of what Phillips had said about protecting a way of life, and wondered what it was about her way of life that had driven a woman to run into the line of fire.

He meant to find out.

CHAPTER 9

After Samantha had exhausted herself in the swimming pool, she and MacKenzie went in search of the only sustenance that could possibly replenish her depleted energy resources: chocolate ice-cream. Luckily for her, an ice-cream van by the name of *The Dairy Dude* stationed itself near the entrance to the holiday park every afternoon, and was a beacon for miles around thanks to its enormous logo featuring a cartoon cow wearing sunglasses.

"Here we are, m'lady," its owner said, and presented Samantha with a towering cone of double chocolate fudge, complete with all the toppings.

"Thanks!" the girl said, and dived straight in.

"Lord help us," MacKenzie said, and was only half-joking.

"Have a good day, ladies!"

The van's owner leaned forward to wave them off. He was around thirty, and what Phillips would have described as 'trendy', with a carefully-tended, designer beard and plenty of tattoos covering his forearms. He wore a yellow t-shirt with the same sunglass-sporting cow printed on the front, and had the tanned look of a man who spent much of his time outdoors.

"See you tomorrow, I expect," MacKenzie said, with an indulgent smile.

It was hard not to spoil Samantha, just a little. For much of her life, she'd been forgotten—if not mistreated, then neglected and starved of love and affection. She hadn't enjoyed holidays by the sea, or splashing in a swimming pool along with the other kids. Denise and

Frank wanted to show her some of those things and begin to build up a store of memories they could look back on, in years to come.

As she made her way back to the campervan with Samantha slurping cheerfully beside her, MacKenzie broached a topic they'd been meaning to discuss for some time.

Now seemed as good a time as any.

"Are you happy living with us, Sam?"

The little girl looked up at her with an ice-cream moustache and a quizzical expression on her face.

"I love living with you and Frank," she said quietly, and then frowned. "Have you changed your mind about having me?"

MacKenzie stopped walking and sank down so they were at eye level, being of the firm belief that all important things in life should be said face-to-face.

She took the girl's shoulders in a gentle grip, and smiled with her whole heart.

"Samantha, having you as part of our family is the greatest privilege of our lives," she said softly. "We've never regretted, for one single moment, having you with us."

The girl smiled beautifully.

"In fact, the reason I asked if you were happy living with us is because Frank and I were wondering if you might like to make it a permanent arrangement. I mean to say, we were hoping you might let us adopt you."

MacKenzie swallowed, feeling suddenly nervous as the girl stared at her with wide green eyes, saying nothing at all.

"I know I'm not your real mum, but I promise to try my best—" she started to say, but was interrupted by the force of the little girl's body as she pressed herself into MacKenzie, wrapping her arms around the woman who'd been more of a mother to her than she'd ever known.

"I love you," Samantha said, her voice muffled against MacKenzie's stomach. "I'd like to be your daughter."

"I love you, too, munchkin," she managed, blinking rapidly to stave off tears as they stood with their arms wrapped around one another, there in the middle of the campsite. "Even without any adoption papers, it feels as though you're already ours."

In that moment, MacKenzie would have fought any battle, waged any war, if only to keep the little girl safe and warm. She'd have travelled any distance and climbed any mountain, if only to keep her from harm. She didn't even mind the fact that the ice cream cone had been smeared somewhere around her posterior.

* * *

Back at the Otterburn Camp, Ryan, Phillips and Major Malloy decided to interview the officers attached to the training exercise in order of rank, beginning at the top. They found the Commanding Officer of the 1st Royal Welsh Fusiliers in his office, which was reserved for the senior ranking officer of whichever company happened to be 'on-base' at the time.

Ryan knocked briefly, then entered.

"Ah, it's my turn, I see?"

Some brief research had elicited the fact that Lieutenant Colonel Theodore Robson—"Teddy", to his friends—had been born and bred in the Scottish borders, not far from Jedburgh. There was little discernible accent, all trace of it having been drummed out during his years at Sandhurst followed by twenty years of living mostly on army bases in the south. He was an imposing and, they supposed, a handsome man, who exercised a good measure of cheerful charisma to offset the duties and responsibilities that went alongside his rank, a fact which made him eminently popular with his troops.

"Come in and have a seat," he invited. "Coffee? Tea? Or, perhaps, something stronger? I know I could use a dram after the morning we've all had."

They settled on coffee, which he made himself using some ground beans and a cafetière.

"Bring this everywhere with me," he said, jiggling the pot in his hand. "Can't stand the weak stuff they serve in the urns."

Ryan couldn't have agreed more—he took a generous gulp of the fragrant liquid and was instantly revived.

"Lieutenant Colonel—"

"Ted, please," he said, with an easy smile.

"Thank you," Ryan said. "I'm not sure if you've met Major Malloy? She'll be joining us in order to keep her own record, for the purposes of a report she'll be compiling for the Defence Accident Investigation Branch. Is that alright with you?"

He spread his hands.

"Happy to be of service, however I can."

"In that case, can you please start by telling us, to the best of your recollection, the events of last night—beginning with your involvement in the strategic planning of the tactical live-fire exercise?" Ryan asked.

Robson leaned back in his chair, settling in for the discussion.

"Well, naturally, the buck for all operations, including tactical exercises, stops with me," he said. "That being said, the actual day-to-day planning of exercises such as the one last night usually falls to my second-in-command, Major Owen Jones, who you met earlier today. He's the Senior Planning Officer with direct oversight of the Range Conducting Officer and his team, who report directly to him."

"So, you had no part in planning the logistics of last night's exercise?" Malloy asked him.

"No, none at all," he said. "Owen ran the final plan by me yesterday afternoon, prior to briefing the troops, and after a full risk assessment had been made. I was pleased to approve it, as it met all the necessary safety guidelines, and so forth."

"Is it usual for troops to conduct night-time exercises like that?" Ryan asked.

Robson nodded.

"Quite normal," he said. "The fact is, we have to train our soldiers to be resilient in all conditions, across all manner of terrain. We do them a disservice, otherwise, when they come to complete their first tour and find themselves unprepared to deal with the demands of warfare."

Ryan consulted his own notebook.

"I understand the training exercise began at around nine o'clock yesterday evening, is that correct?"

"I believe so."

"Would you mind telling us what your own movements were, around that time?"

Robson's eyebrows shot into his buzz cut.

"Ah, chief inspector, I have nothing to hide, but I'm curious to know why my movements should interest you, given that I was not one of the firers at the time of the incident?"

Ryan smiled genially.

"It's purely routine, sir. We like to have a full and complete picture."

Robson spread his hands again.

"In that case, I'm afraid I was enjoying a terribly unremarkable Friday night here in my quarters, with a good book," he said. "I believe I nodded off sometime after ten, and was awakened at five-twenty, give or take five minutes, by the Company Sergeant Major, Gwen Davies, who banged on my door around then."

47

"Which book was it?" Phillips asked, and Robson turned to face him.

"Which book was what?"

"The one you were reading, last night," Phillips reminded him.

"It was *Tinker, Tailor, Soldier, Spy,*" Robson replied. "One of the classic spy novels, in my opinion."

"After you were alerted to the incident, what happened then?" Ryan asked.

"I got over there, as quickly as I could," he replied. "The emergency services had already been called, so I drove along with the Company Sergeant Major to the site near Witch Crags and arranged for a transport vehicle to follow, in order to take the section back to the Base. It took around fifteen minutes to reach the same access point via road as you saw, earlier today."

"At around five forty-five, would you say?"

"Yes, that sounds right."

"Who did you see, when you arrived by the road access, near Linshiels Lake?"

"The RCO, 2nd Lieutenant Pat Dalgliesh, was there with the Medical Officer, Rupert Sanderson, and Corporal Rhys Evans. They were supervising the casualty, who had by that time been transferred by stretcher to the roadside to enable the emergency services to gain better access. I understand Lieutenant Jones remained with Corporal Huxley and the section troops, who were seated with their backs to the casualty at that time."

Ryan nodded.

"And, was it your understanding that the victim was dead, or alive, by that time?"

"It was quite clear that she had, most regrettably, died."

"Did you recognise her, at all?"

Robson was bemused.

"Certainly not, although, it must be said, I was unable to—well, you know. It was hard to distinguish particular features."

"What was she wearing?" Phillips asked, and Robson was thrown off-guard.

"Wearing? I—goodness, I'm not sure I remember. Let me see, now. I seem to recall being able to see her legs, so she must have been wearing quite a short skirt. I'm sorry, I can't remember what it looked like. Her injuries were too extensive to discern much in the way of detail, and it was still reasonably dark."

"Do you have your own theory of what happened?"

Robson cupped his coffee mug between his hands and shook his head.

"It grieves me to say it, but I think we have here a very tragic case of somebody finding themselves in the wrong place, at the wrong time. However, and for whatever reason that unfortunate woman happened to find herself in the pathway of a live-fire exercise, it would have been almost impossible for any of our troops to distinguish her from a moving target. They're designed to simulate a real person, and are thermal to replicate the heat radiating from a human body. In the absence of any external light source, it's small wonder Private Stephenson mistook the woman for the target."

"You believe then, that Private Stephenson was probably responsible for firing the first shot?" Malloy asked.

Robson held up his hands.

"I've had an opportunity to listen to a recording of last night's exercise and, although Stephenson was the one to sound the attack, that isn't to say she was the one to fire the shot that killed the woman; in the army, we're one for all."

And all for one, Ryan thought.

"How do you account for the presence of a civilian on the training range?"

"I think it's clear that the woman was lost, and somehow managed to miss the red flags. Admittedly, they're harder to see, at night. I can't say I know what she was doing wandering around at that hour, but perhaps she'd been staying in a shepherd's bothy, or something of that sort. The territory attracts wanderers and poets, so I'm told."

"Not all who wander are lost," Ryan murmured, with the ghost of a smile. "But we'll bear your theory in mind."

CHAPTER 10

Beneath the concrete flyover, the soldier huddled into his sleeping bag and pressed the heels of his hands to his ears. The traffic overhead had picked up so there was a constant whirr of engines and, to his addled mind, they sounded like army drones, flying through the sky like giant, angry wasps as they prepared to strike.

"Need a couple of quid, mate?"

He recognised the voice and wished he could curl up even tighter; he wished he could make himself so small, he'd be invisible.

A moment later, a hand reached out to tug the sleeping bag away from his face and he found himself staring up into a pair of friendly blue eyes.

But looks were deceptive.

Alfie Rodgers was a poor excuse for a human being. He was well aware of the fact and had not spent any time mourning, or considering how the situation might be improved; his brain never having developed the crucial components that were required, if one was to feel empathy for one's fellow man.

"There he is!" Alfie crooned, and the stooge who had accompanied him on his rounds of the city let out the rasping laugh of one who smoked at least twenty fags a day.

The soldier said nothing.

He'd learned, the first time, not to answer back. It was funny, he supposed, that a man of his combat abilities should feel fear in the face of the little runt, but it was just another measure of how far he had fallen. Besides, Alfie didn't work alone. He had a network of messengers and enforcers, any of whom could come and find him in the long hours of the night, if he wasn't careful.

"How you doin', pal?" Alfie asked, coming down on his haunches so he could speak softly to his next mark. "I've gotta be honest, you don't look so good. You look as if you need a little pick me up."

Again, the soldier said nothing.

Not even when Alfie scanned both directions of the underpass, and then pulled out a small plastic pouch.

"Look at this, mate. Why don't you try a bit of spice? It'll perk you right up, I promise."

The soldier's eyes darted to the pouch—just once—and then back into the watchful eyes of the predator who'd been hunting him for weeks, now.

"I'll do you a deal," Alfie whispered. "You take an ounce or two, now, and you don't have to pay me for it just yet. We're mates, aren't we? Mates help each other out, don't they?"

The soldier thought back to the poppy fields in Helmand Province, and of the lives that had been lost, then looked back at the small plastic pouch.

"I'm going to tuck this safely in here," Alfie said, and reached out to put the pouch inside the sleeping bag.

The soldier's hand shot out, and caught the teenager's wrist.

"I don't want your bloody drugs," he growled. "Leave me alone."

Alfie's expression never wavered. His smooth face continued to smile, and his eyes maintained the same innocent quality that served him so well in his chosen profession. Whilst some of the other kids at school were talking about becoming contestants on *Love Island*, he'd always known he was destined for greater things. With his business acumen and superlative people skills, he planned to run his own empire, one day.

But, in the meantime, he was building his business, one customer at a time.

"Let's have a little chat about this tomorrow," he suggested, and then surprised himself by dropping a handful of loose change in the cracked cup sitting next to the soldier's cup. "Go on, have a burger, on me."

The soldier heard their footsteps echoing through the underpass and breathed a sigh of relief that, this time, there had been no violence. He was still sore from the kicking he'd received from a crowd of drunken students, the night before, and his body needed time to heal.

Just then, he heard more footsteps approaching; faster than the last, and accompanied by the scratch of claws against the concrete floor.

The dog buried its face in his sleeping bag and sniffed him.

Then, sat back and waited.

"Go away," the soldier said, half-heartedly this time. "Why do you keep coming back here? I don't have anything for you."

The dog continued to look at him with shiny brown eyes, and then it flattened its belly against the floor. After another minute passed, it shuffled closer, nosing its way towards him an inch at a time.

Until he felt the dog's warm body curving against his own, and the warm puff of its breath against his skin.

"I don't—" he tried to say, over the hitching of his own breath. "I don't want you."

But his hands came around the dog's warm body and held on, and the animal's tongue licked the salty tears from his face as they clung together in the shadows of the city.

* * *

In the barracks at Otterburn Training Camp, the mood was sombre.

Conversation stopped when Private Jess Stephenson returned to her bunk, and she saw the awkward looks from her fellow trainees.

They knew it was her fault.

It *was* her fault.

She lay her head on the pillow and curled up, wishing she had something to cling to through the long hours of the night.

CHAPTER 11

As evening began to draw in, Ryan, Phillips and Malloy decided to conduct one final interview before calling it a day, and went in search of the Medical Officer, Major Rupert Sanderson.

They found him in his office, drafting up his notes from the events of the morning.

"Come in!"

They entered a small, clinical office space very much like the one they might have found at their local GP surgery, with a consulting table, locked supplies cupboard and a corner desk where Sanderson was presently seated. He was a conservative man of around forty, with distinctive, curly salt-and-pepper grey hair and small, myopic eyes. He'd spent the first few years of his professional life as a doctor, with a regular stream of patients as a General Practitioner, before deciding to enlist as an army officer. Since then, he'd completed two tours in Iraq and Afghanistan, and they could be fairly sure he'd seen more than his fair share of human destruction.

"Sorry to disturb you," Ryan said. "We met earlier; I'm DCI Ryan and this is DS Phillips, from Northumbria CID, and Major Malloy, of the Defence AIB."

Sanderson turned around in his chair.

"Right, yes. I suppose you'll need to ask me some questions?"

Ryan nodded.

"Take a seat, if you can find one."

Ryan offered the only spare seat to Major Malloy, who wondered for a moment whether his chivalry masked a deeper level of male chauvinism, before realising the gesture was gender-neutral; he had the kind of ingrained manners that led him to put others before himself.

And, as it happened, her feet were just starting to ache.

"Thank you," she said.

Ryan turned back to the doctor.

"We'll be asking these questions under caution, but that's entirely normal," he said. "If you'd like to have a lawyer present, you're entitled, but it's not necessary. We're looking to build up a picture of the sequence of events."

"I quite understand," Sanderson said, in the clipped tones Ryan recognised all too well from his days at boarding school. "I'm perfectly happy to answer whatever questions you might have."

"Could you start by telling us whether you were in attendance throughout the training exercise?"

Sanderson nodded.

"Yes, I was there throughout. It's protocol, in case of injury— normally, it's a case of sprained ankles and the occasional broken bone."

"Unfortunately, not in this instance," Ryan said. "When did you first become aware that the section had engaged a live target, as opposed to the mechanised one they intended to find?"

Sanderson removed his glasses, and began to polish them on the edge of his trousers.

"I was actually just drafting my own notes on this topic," he admitted. "I believe I first became aware at around quarter past five this morning. That's when I first heard one of the firers shouting 'TARGET CENTRE', or something similar. I was already privy to the planned exercise, and I knew that the target was located at least another half a mile or so further north of that position."

"What happened when you heard the firer giving the battle cry?"

"Myself and 2nd Lieutenant Dalgliesh were located on higher ground to the east of the firers, and Pat—as RCO on the exercise—called out the order for them to stop."

"And did they?"

"Yes, but not immediately. They responded incredibly quickly to a perceived target, and immediately engaged in a 'fire and move' formation."

"What's that, when it's at home?" Phillips asked, and drew a reluctant smile from the doctor.

"It's a standard attack strategy, where soldiers walking in a horizontal line formation split into three to confront the target. Firers from each end of the line peel away and move at speed, around the sides of the target, while those in the centre of the line maintain a forward advance position and continue to fire."

"And you're saying they'd already engaged the target, before the RCO was able to call them off?"

"That's correct. As I say, they acted very swiftly."

"What happened, once the section ceased firing?" Ryan asked.

"We could see through our own thermal vision that a live target had been hit. We were around a hundred yards away, on the sloping edge of the hillside on the western edge of the valley. Amanda—that's Corporal Huxley—was the security officer on the ground, following around fifty yards behind the firers in the section. She ran across, while we hurried down the hill. I believe Huxley and Dalgliesh told the firers to lock their weapons and place them on the ground, alongside their packs. I went straight across to attend to the casualty, where I found Private Stephenson standing nearby."

Ryan looked up at that.

"She wasn't with the others?"

"No. She seemed extremely distressed, but I'm afraid I had no opportunity to tend to her. I can't remember whether it was Dalgliesh or Huxley, but one of them told her to return to the rest of her section, whilst we called the emergency services and assessed the casualty."

"And, turning now to the casualty, how did you find her?" Ryan asked.

Sanderson spoke in the detached voice that many clinicians developed in the early days of their careers when dealing with, and speaking of, severe trauma. Ryan recognised it instantly, having cultivated something very similar, himself.

"Whilst the lighting was very poor, I can tell you the casualty appeared to be a young woman, somewhere between the ages of eighteen and thirty, or thereabouts. She had sustained a gunshot wound to the head. Although we reached her no more than a couple of minutes after she fell, I could find no pulse."

He paused to collect his thoughts.

"In accordance with procedure, I administered CPR until the decision was taken to move her closer to the road, by stretcher, which I had with me."

He paused to take a sip of water.

"In your view, is there anything that could have prevented the incident from occurring?" Malloy asked. "Any measures the Army could put in place, that were lacking on the field last night and into this morning?"

Sanderson gave the question proper consideration, and then shook his head.

"It was a perfect storm," he said, sadly. "I don't think there's any way we could have prevented it. The woman just seemed to appear from nowhere. Perhaps, if it had been a daytime exercise…"

He trailed off.

"Thank you, Doctor," Ryan murmured, and thought that the victim's family would be glad to know that, even when all hope appeared to be lost, this man had still tried to save her.

CHAPTER 12

It was after six by the time Ryan and Phillips departed Otterburn Training Camp; Phillips to return to his family in Wooler, and Ryan to make the short journey back to Elsdon. As the sun dipped lower in the sky, a thin veil of mist began to descend over the moors, curling its way over the tufts of heather and gorse, lending a sepia hue to the landscape that might have come straight out of a postcard.

Ryan was dimly aware of the passing scenery, but his mind was occupied elsewhere as he ruminated on one interesting point that had come out of their interviews with the officers who attended the exercise the night before.

Why had Private Stephenson approached what she believed to be a mechanical target—unless she was already aware it was a live target?

And, if she was aware, why had she not called off the attack, or put down her weapon before firing?

These were questions worth thinking about, because they went to motive. There was a great deal of difference between an 'accidental' death, where a soldier acting in the line of his or her duty accidentally kills a civilian, and a 'suspicious' death, where there is some element of premeditation, or what the law liked to call *mens rea*. It would be all too easy for him to sign off the death as accidental without properly considering the alternative, because his natural presumption was that soldiers killed only in the line of duty.

But that was not always the case.

There had been ample opportunity to begin gathering evidence about the camp and its inhabitants, but considerably less opportunity to learn about the victim. In Ryan's experience, that was infinitely more valuable to a police investigation; for instance, they might just find that, contrary to their statements, the unknown woman was known to one of those brandishing a weapon that morning.

On the other hand, the remorse of each of the six firers had seemed genuine; in particular, Private Stephenson, who was convinced she was responsible for the woman's death.

Soon, he reached the historic village of Elsdon, with its quaint stone houses and pele tower, and felt a sense of calm begin to descend, as it did each time he returned to the home he and Anna had made together. The house they'd built was at the top of a hill, accessed by a narrow, single-track lane flanked by tall hedgerows on either side, and boasted panoramic views of the valley. He considered himself a very lucky man, but he'd have lived in a shack in the woods, so long as they were together.

It was a warm evening, and he found his wife sitting outside, on the terrace at the back of the house. A half-full glass of white wine rested on a small table beside her, and she'd kicked off her shoes to wriggle her toes in the grass. In her hands, she held a sketchbook and a charcoal pencil, which she was using to make sweeping marks on the page.

Anna paused when she heard him step out onto the patio.

"Hello," she said, setting aside the sketchbook to walk over and greet him. "I wasn't expecting you for another couple of hours. I know how it is, when you land a new case."

She curved her arms around his neck and drew him in for a lingering kiss.

"I missed you," he said.

The Criminal Investigation Department had enjoyed a rare period of calm, following a major drugs bust at the start of the summer. That had resulted in the disbanding of a dangerous gang, the toppling of its leader and any number of his network of dealers, messengers, enforcers and runners—but it had also opened up a Pandora's Box of professional standards misdemeanours and corruption for the constabulary to deal with. Nobody liked a clean house more than Ryan, but uncovering all the backhanders and kickbacks had wrought a human cost in terms of increased workload and bureaucracy he and his team had worked tirelessly to clear.

Now that the process was almost complete, and the Crown Prosecution Service had taken over the necessary files, he and his team were free to return to their usual order of business; namely, murder, rape and all the other serious crimes one person was capable of inflicting upon another.

"What's the case about?" Anna asked, and offered him the other half of her wine.

Ryan took a sip and gave her an executive summary of his day, without going into any specifics, while they took a seat on the wicker sofa overlooking the garden.

"As soon as I've spoken to the pathologist and the ballistics team, tomorrow morning, I'll be in a position to determine whether the death was suspicious," he said. "Until then, it's looking like a tragic accident."

"It's sadder still that nobody knows who she was," Anna murmured. "Hasn't anybody been reported missing?"

Ryan shook his head.

"Not anybody matching her description, and nobody in the past week."

He paused, frowning off into the distance, and she ran a gentle hand over his back.

"Hey, are you okay?"

He pulled her close again, drawing strength from her warmth, and rubbed his cheek against her soft hair.

"I keep asking myself why she was there in the first place, and why she was running," he muttered. "Then, there's her clothing, and the fact nobody's reported her missing."

"You're worried," Anna realised.

"Yes," he said. "I'm very worried. I've got a terrible feeling we're only just scratching the surface, and the real investigation is about to begin."

* * *

Over the hills in Wooler, Phillips had already been enlisted for the next investigation.

The Mysterious Case of the Missing Horseshoe was, according to its poster, a 'theatrical triumph', written by and starring a travelling amateur dramatic society who had decided to make their base at the holiday camp for the season. Samantha had been eager to see the play since their first day of arrival and, until today, Phillips and MacKenzie had been able to distract her.

However, they had known all along they were merely putting off the inevitable.

And so, Frank and Denise found themselves seated in the front row of the small auditorium, armed to the teeth with overpriced programmes, tubs of ice-cream from *The Dairy Dude* and the kind of stoical, wartime mentality Churchill would have been proud of.

"How much longer will this go on?" MacKenzie hissed, and earned herself a playful jab in the ribs from Samantha.

"Shh!" she said. "I'm trying to work out if it was the butler."

"It's always the doctor," Phillips said, sagely.

"*Shh!*" somebody else said, in the row behind.

"Alreet, man, wind yer neck in," Phillips muttered, and folded his arms across his paunch.

He glanced across at the enraptured face of the little girl seated beside him and smiled. If he was stuck there until the bitter end, he could think of worse people to share his time in captivity with than two lovely redheads.

He reached across and took MacKenzie's hand and held it in his own, until the very end.

CHAPTER 13

DC Melanie Yates' new flat was located on the first floor of a small, purpose-built apartment block in an area of Newcastle known as 'Fenham'. It was a nice part of town adjacent to the Town Moor; a large, green common where they'd recently been called in to investigate murder within a circus community, and where MacKenzie and Phillips had first met their new foster daughter, Samantha. Murder notwithstanding, the Moor was an airy green space where city-dwellers such as herself could go for a pleasant walk on their days off.

She and Jack had decided to share a takeaway pizza and a bottle of wine in her cosy new surroundings. Jack preferred it to his own apartment, which now held so many negative memories it no longer felt like home, and she was happy to share her space with him since they were enjoying one another's company so much.

It had been a long road, she thought, but they'd made it there in the end.

Once they'd toed off their shoes and settled themselves on her new L-shaped sofa with a slice of double cheese pizza in hand, talk turned to the events of the day.

They'd spent much of their time interviewing witnesses and speaking with the imam, whose sadness at the loss of the Central Mosque had been matched only by his forgiveness of those who had set the fire which, the Fire Investigator had told them, had almost certainly been started by the use of a small incendiary device posted through the letterbox adjacent to the main doors. It would take time for its components to be analysed, and even more time to investigate when, where and in what quantities those components had been bought, and by whom—assuming, of course, that the components were distinguishable from everyday household items and could be traced at all.

"With the first attack on the synagogue last week, they used a bit of petrol and some fire starters," Jack said. "It was a botched job, because the flames didn't take hold. It caused some superficial damage, but probably not to the extent they were hoping for."

"They upgraded their technique, this time, you mean?"

"If it's the same people," Jack shrugged, and took another bite of pizza. "The symbol spray-painted on the walls of the synagogue and the mosque is the same, but it might have been different members of the same organisation who perpetrated each crime—could account for the difference in MO."

Melanie nodded.

"Is it a neo-Nazi symbol, do you think?"

"I think it's an ancient Nordic symbol," Jack replied. "I haven't had much of a chance to research it, properly. I was hoping we could ask Anna about it, since she's a bit of an expert on religious symbology in these parts."

As an academic historian specialising in ancient pagan religious practices, Ryan's wife and their mutual friend was a fount of knowledge.

"I'll give her a call tomorrow and see if she has a few minutes to spare."

There was a short pause, while they each chewed contentedly.

"Religion has a lot to answer for," Jack remarked. "So does politics, for that matter. I've never known the country to be so divided. It's the perfect breeding ground for extremism."

"I think you mean, *people* have a lot to answer for," she said, with a wry smile. "People can find anything to justify their cause, if they look hard enough. There have always been divides, but it comes down to human nature. Some people look for conflict and others try to avoid it."

The pizza now finished, Jack reached over to slide an arm around her shoulders.

"I hope nothing will divide us, ever again," he said.

Melanie cupped his face with a tender hand.

"So long as you don't keep leaving my toilet seat up, nothing ever will," she said, sweetly.

* * *

Night-time was the hardest.

The soldier knew they'd come for him again, once the sun went down and the crowds went home. At the moment, the streets were swollen with Friday night revellers who chattered by in swanky clothes and painted faces as they made their way towards the bars and clubs. He watched them go by and thought he must have seen every kind of shoe, and every kind of person.

Now and then, somebody stopped to throw a penny into his cracked cup and, once or twice, somebody left a cold sandwich and a cup of lukewarm tea—usually, while he was asleep, so they didn't have to speak to him. He appreciated the sentiment, all the same.

He was getting pretty good at being able to predict which category a person would fall into.

There were the 'do-gooders' and the 'missionaries'; the 'ramblers', the 'druggies' and the 'fighters' but, perhaps most of all, he hated the 'philosophers'.

And he could see one coming over right now.

"Alreet, mate?"

This one had a girl on his arm, the soldier noticed. That meant he was making an effort to appear socially conscious, to impress her.

He grunted.

"How'd you end up on the streets, then? Was it the drugs?"

He eyed the man, with his perma-tanned face and dyed black hair, his whitened teeth and his over-tight jeans, and felt a surge of hatred.

"I've never taken that shit," he muttered, and instantly regretted opening his mouth. Any conversation would fuel a philosopher, who loved nothing more than the sound of his own wind-bagging voice.

"Howay, man, I'm not judgin' yer," he said, glancing back towards the girl, who swayed slightly on four-inch heels. "I just wanna get to know you."

He said nothing.

"What happened to yer face, like? Get caught in a fire?"

His scarred skin prickled, as he remembered the flames. The scent of his own body burning...

"Have you got any spare change?" the soldier asked, cutting to the chase. Hunger trumped pride, and the soup kitchen wasn't open that night.

The philosopher made an elaborate show of patting his pockets and then pulled an apologetic face.

"Sorry, feller, I've got nowt on me. Take care of yourself, yeah?"

They left quickly, and didn't look back.

* * *

Private Jess Stephenson couldn't wait any longer. She couldn't just lie there, wondering and worrying.

She'd go mad.

As one of only three women in her platoon, Jess had the female bunkroom all to herself. Now that the other two had taken themselves off to the local pub, in Otterburn, it was deserted.

The sky was darkening quickly, and, in another hour, it would be pitch black, just as it was the previous night when they'd first set out on their ill-fated training exercise.

Her hands trembled again, and she clasped them around her waist to try to stop it.

When night fell, she'd try to slip out.

She had to know for sure.

She thought again of the dead woman's hands, and her breath lodged in her chest as she imagined them reaching out to touch her, to tangle in her hair…

Tears leaked from the corners of her eyes, and she let them come.

* * *

Once darkness had fallen, the van made its way over the desolate countryside, following the road from Wooler to Town Yetholm, on the other side of the border. Occasionally, it passed through a village or hamlet, but the streets were empty of cars or people at that hour; most having tucked themselves away safely in their beds.

Or so they believed.

There was a sliver of moon that night, and occasional shafts of silvery light broke through the clouds to illuminate the solitary vehicle as it crawled its way up and over the hills to Scotland. When the clouds shifted again, darkness fell like a shroud, and was relieved only by the twin beams of the van's headlights as it motored further away from home.

The *purr* of the van's engine broke into the silent evening as it climbed steep inclines and was suspended for a moment, before racing down the other side. Its driver tried not to become too excited by the evening's hunt; success depended upon careful planning and secrecy, above all else.

The van kept to a reasonable speed—not too fast, not too slow—and didn't pass a soul until it reached the border.

Suddenly, it appeared.

The garish lights of a small, twenty-four-hour service station called to him, beckoning him closer.

But he didn't drive to the main entrance.

Oh, no.

He drove to the back, beyond the truck stops and the rubbish bins, to a cold and dusty patch of soil where he knew she would be waiting. A woman who had already sacrificed herself, and all she was, for money.

Now, he'd teach her the true value of life.

CHAPTER 14

Saturday 17ᵗʰ August 2019

It was almost three a.m. when Private Becky Grainger and Private Sarah Abbott stumbled back to the dorm. Leave might have been cancelled that weekend, but that didn't stop them enjoying the finest pale ales the pubs of Otterburn had to offer, nor from enjoying a quick fumble in the dark with a couple of the local boys.

Becky was about to turn on the light, when her friend stopped her.

"You'll wake *Jessh*," she slurred, and then giggled at herself.

They liked their roommate and fellow squaddie well enough, but she was far too serious—Jess Stephenson spent all her free time visiting her boyfriend back in Cardiff or reading her bloody current affairs books. She never came down for a pint at the pub or put on a bit of slap and a pair of heels. They might be soldiers, but they were entitled to have a laugh.

"She's not here," Sarah said, in a stage whisper. "She's not in her bed."

"Maybe she's in the loo," Becky yawned, and kicked off her shoes before flopping down onto her bunk.

Sarah wandered in that direction, since she needed it herself, and was about to tell her friend that

Jess wasn't in there, either, when she found Becky fast asleep and snoring on top of her covers. She glanced over at Jessica's empty bunk and wondered if she should tell someone, and then thought better of it.

If Jess wanted to cheat on her boyfriend, she wouldn't be the one to rat her out. She'd just have to give her all the gory details in the morning, that was all.

With a huge, jaw-cracking yawn, Sarah tumbled onto her own bed and was asleep within minutes.

* * *

When Becky and Sarah awakened the following morning, Jess was still nowhere to be seen.

"Never thought she had it in her," Becky admitted, with a bawdy chuckle. "She seems all prim and proper."

Sarah made a murmuring sound of agreement as she wiped away the mascara smeared beneath her eyes, and then frowned.

"It really doesn't seem like her," she said, eventually. "I dunno, Becks. I wonder if she's okay."

"She's probably bangin' Lieutenant Love-Nuts, as we speak," her friend replied, and sent them both into peals of laughter.

"I'm *serious*," Sarah said again. "She seemed in a right funny mood, after what happened yesterday."

"Well she would be, wouldn't she? Maybe she needed some light relief from it all."

"She goes on about that boyfriend of hers like he's God's gift," Sarah said, with just a touch of envy. "I can't see her throwin' it all to the wind, can you?"

"Maybe she's thinkin' he won't find out."

"You're *terrible*, you are!"

* * *

It was shortly after nine o'clock in the morning when Jessica Stephenson's roommates decided to report her missing. After all reasonable attempts were made to contact her by phone, and a quick search of the main buildings turned up no sign of her, a search party was assembled, and the police were informed.

Ryan took the call as he and Phillips stood beneath a thin plastic canopy outside the service entrance to the mortuary, at the Royal Victoria Infirmary in Newcastle.

"Did you hear that?" Ryan asked his sergeant. "Private Jess Stephenson is missing."

Phillips was concerned.

"She was in a bad way, yesterday," he said. "Poor lass, I hope she hasn't gone and done something stupid. Even if she *was* the one to call out the target, she can't be blamed for acting on orders—that's a soldier's job."

Ryan agreed.

"They've got the whole barracks combing the area for her as we speak," he said. "I told them we'd get up there, as soon as we've spoken with the pathologist."

"Aye, let's have a word with Pinter and be on our way," Phillips said. "Hopefully, he'll have some answers for us."

Doctor Jeffrey Pinter was the Chief Pathologist attached to Northumbria CID, and one of the best in the country. He was a tall, mildly eccentric man, whose bony features and pale skin seemed uniquely suited to his work environment. Despite the sombre nature of his profession, he was known to be a cheerful sort of man, with a penchant for seventies soul classics, which he often played on the Bluetooth speakers he'd fitted in each corner of the wide, open-plan space at his own expense.

There was no music today, however—when Ryan and Phillips made their way along a stiflingly hot corridor and keyed themselves through the large security doors leading into the mortuary, they found their colleague in a grave sort of mood.

No pun intended.

"Morning, Jeff," Ryan said, after he'd scrawled their names into the logbook. "Thanks for coming in on your day off."

"It's alright, I had nothing better to do," he grumbled. "It's been a slow week, as it happens."

"You've got a face like a slapped arse this mornin', Jeff," Phillips declared. "What ails you? Here, how's things with that lass—what was her name again?"

"Joanne," Pinter said, wistfully. "And, if you must know, she's away this weekend. She's taken Archie to Center Parcs for some mother-son time before he starts back at school."

Though he was a decent, hardworking man, until recent times Jeff Pinter's love life would not have been the stuff of romance novels or—better yet—the stuff of *erotic* novels. However, their crusty friend had been fortunate to have found what might prove to be the only woman in the world to find forensic pathology sexy, owing largely to the fact she was of the same profession herself. The luminous Joanne was a forty-two-year-old divorcee with a young son by the name of Archie, and Pinter was still finding his feet in the unexpected role of stepfather, amongst other things.

"Cheer up, Casanova," Ryan said. "She'll be back soon enough."

Pinter heaved a lovesick sigh, which was plainly ridiculous for a man of his age and hair loss, and then turned to the matters in hand.

"Right, let me take you to see the lady who came in yesterday," he said, leading them through the main mortuary space towards a corridor at the end leading to a number of private examination rooms that were reserved for special cases, such as these.

Pinter buzzed through the smaller security door, then led them along a whitewashed corridor to Examination Room C. There was a stronger scent of chemicals towards that end of the corridor, mingled with the sickly sweet, over-ripe scent of death that was unique in nature.

"She's in here," he told them, then paused with his hand on the door knob and gave them a serious look. "We've seen a lot of things in our time, and some of it's been very bad. I think I should tell you, this is one of those times."

It was never at the top of anybody's wish list to take a trip to the mortuary, but it was a necessary part of getting to know the victim and the crime. It was often hard and unpleasant, but they kept coming back because they remembered one thing: the victim could not speak, but their body was perhaps the greatest clue to finding their killer or, in this case, to understanding how they'd come to find themselves in such a vulnerable position.

"We're ready," Ryan said, and Phillips ordered his stomach to retain the contents of his last meal as the door swung open.

An examination table stood in the centre of the room, which was purposefully chilled since the body had been taken out of its freezer compartment. Overhead, strip lighting shone an eerie, greyish-white glow thanks to a bulk order of energy-saving bulbs from the hospital store. A shrouded figure lay on the table, covered in a long paper sheet that didn't quite reach her toes.

Though she had since been washed and cleaned, Ryan noticed that the undersides of both of her feet were severely bruised and covered in lacerations.

"Did she come in with any shoes?" he asked, before Pinter could reach for the paper covering.

"No, as a matter of fact, she didn't. Sometimes, people come in without footwear if the paramedics have removed them, or they've been lost sometime during the recovery process. However, looking at the condition of this lady's feet, I'd say it's more likely she hadn't been wearing any for some time prior to the incident."

"Must've hurt like hell," Phillips said, gruffly.

"Are you both ready?" Pinter asked, and, at their nod, he removed the paper shroud.

There was absolute silence in the small room as each man accustomed himself to what lay before him. The remains of what had once been a blonde-haired woman, around five feet six inches tall, rested on the examination table. Her face was torn beyond recognition, and what remained bore the ugly mark of a surgeon's dark thread.

"I removed the bullet," Pinter said quietly. "Ballistics say they'll get back to us this morning with an update, since you asked for a rush on it."

Ryan nodded. The resources weren't always available for an express service from the specialist forensic units attached to CID but, in this case, the Ministry of Defence had approved a supplementary budget to enable the swift and smooth handling of one of their own.

He only wished every unfortunate soul who found themselves laid bare on Pinter's operating table was afforded the same fast service; if not for their own sake, for the sake of those who were left behind to mourn them.

"What can you tell us about the body?"

Ryan ventured closer to the cadaver and peered through the bulging plastic bags covering the woman's hands to see if they could tell him something—anything—about the person she had once been.

"Well, for starters, I can tell you she must have clambered over rocks and all kinds," Pinter said. "Her fingertips were shredded, and several nails were torn. I've sampled them, as usual, and I'll let you know if anything interesting comes of it."

Ryan nodded.

"She was also sexually active," Pinter said, flushing a bit as he always did when the topic arose. "There was evidence of fairly recent sexual activity, in fact—I'd say sometime during the past forty-eight hours. I've taken samples from the vaginal wall, but there's unlikely to be anything of particular use owing to the time lag."

"Cause of death is simply catastrophic head injury caused by the gunshot," Pinter said, for good form. He paused. "That said, I did find a small anomaly."

CHAPTER 15

A full company of soldiers from the 1st Royal Welsh Fusiliers, consisting of three platoons totalling ninety men and women—not counting standing officers based at Otterburn Camp—approached the task of searching for one of their number with the same level of military precision they would have employed during any major skirmish around the world. On Ryan's orders, local police forces took up the responsibility of searching the towns and villages in the vicinity, as well as any bus services that had been running through the early hours of the morning, so the army could focus its attention on the more difficult terrain of the Northumberland National Park. They reasoned that, since her roommates had first noticed her absence at around three o'clock, Private Jess Stephenson had had up to seven hours in which to walk, hitchhike or otherwise procure a vehicle. Given the general consensus about her state of mind following the incident the day before, both army and police agreed that she was unlikely to have absconded for nefarious reasons and was more likely to have gone missing in order to inflict self-harm, or to return to the scene of yesterday's incident. Unfortunately, it was too soon to receive any communications data from Stephenson's mobile phone provider to help to narrow down her location, and so they relied upon more old-fashioned methods of search and rescue.

1st and 2nd Platoons were deployed to the west and northern sectors of the Controlled Area, whilst 3rd Platoon—Stephenson's own—focused their search on the south-eastern sector, which included the incident site near Witch Crags and Linshiels Lake. In all, their search aimed to cover ninety square miles of territory, and might have taken several days.

In the event, the search party found Private Jess Stephenson within twenty minutes of leaving the military base, hanging from one of the scented pine trees in a small patch of woodland, less than half a mile away from Witch Crags.

* * *

"You said there was an anomaly?"

Phillips had no intention of hanging around the mortuary for any longer than necessary, so he chivvied things along.

"Ah, yes," Pinter said. "Well, I was going to say that, in previous military cases I've dealt with, the bullets have always been the standard army calibre, which is 5.56mm."

Ryan looked up from his inspection of the woman's injuries, and felt a funny, prescient feeling of dread.

"And in this case?" he asked.

"Well, that was the strange thing about it," Pinter said. "This bullet was a different calibre—most likely from a hunting rifle. A .308 Winchester, I'd say, although ballistics will confirm."

Phillips looked sharply at his friend.

"All the firers were using the same standard-issue army rifle," he said. "The SA80. None of them was carrying a hunting rifle."

Pinter looked between the pair of them and understood the gravity of the information he'd given them.

"You're saying—?"

"There was another shooter on the moors on the night this woman died," Ryan said, and his eyes turned flat and hard. "Yes, exactly."

"I hope to God that lass hasn't done anything," Phillips muttered. "If she went off, thinking she was responsible, when she wasn't—"

Just then, Ryan's phone began to ring, echoing loudly around the confined space. The other two listened tensely as he conducted a short conversation with the person at the other end of the line, Phillips' heart sinking as he watched his friend's face take on a distant, shuttered expression he recognised only too well as being an omen of bad news.

Sure enough, he was right.

Ryan ended the call, and looked at the other two men in the room with blazing eyes the colour of the North Sea, and just as cold.

"They found Private Stephenson," he said flatly. "She's dead."

* * *

As Ryan and Phillips drove back to Otterburn with all speed, Lowerson and Yates made their way to the picturesque city of Durham, thirteen miles further south of Newcastle. It was an ancient, World Heritage Site, with a towering Norman cathedral not dissimilar to the one at Notre Dame, and a smaller but equally impressive castle built sometime during the eleventh century. The city had been built on high ground with the River Wear running at its feet, its babbling waters having provided the backdrop for many a romantic stroll for Ryan and Anna, and countless others who had walked its scenic riverbanks.

"We should go for a wander along the river, if we have time," Yates suggested, as she tucked her car into a tight parking spot with practised ease.

It was on the tip of his tongue to remind her of their hectic work schedule, but recent events had taught him several valuable lessons about what was truly important in life, and about which commodities could never be bought.

Time was one of them.

He'd never be able to relive the moment again, so he should grab it with both hands, while he could.

"I'd love to go for a walk with you, Mel. We should have finished our meeting with Anna by lunchtime—we can grab a sandwich and take it along to one of the benches opposite the cathedral, if you like."

She beamed at him, and then leaned over to give him a smacking kiss.

"Let's go and see if Anna's office has a coffee machine."

"Excellent plan."

Doctor Anna Taylor-Ryan was an eminent local historian with several publications to her name, and she held a senior teaching post in the history faculty at the University of Durham, where she taught three days a week. The other two days were spent researching and writing her next book.

Lowerson and Yates were sometimes guilty of forgetting this aspect of Anna's character, not only because she also happened to be Ryan's wife, but because she was frequently too modest to discuss her exploits in that area. But, as they climbed the steep cobbled streets of the city centre and wound their way up towards College Green, which was the main square beside the cathedral and the castle, they were forcibly reminded that this was a highly academic centre of learning—and their friend was a key part of that.

They found Anna in her office at the History Faculty, which was a pretty old building one street over from College Green. Being a lover of all things quaint and charming, it was fitting that her office was located up a small, spiral staircase with spectacular views of the cathedral through its mullioned windows.

Lowerson tapped the brass plaque on the wall outside, wriggled his eyebrows at Melanie, and then raised his knuckles to rap against the heavy old door.

Anna opened it herself, and grinned at the pair of them.

"You found me, then? Come on in," she said. "Do you fancy a coffee, or is that a daft question?"

Once they were fortified with steaming hot mugs of the good stuff, Lowerson and Yates sank into a small leather sofa that was tucked against one of the walls and which Anna used when conducting smaller tutorial groups with her students.

"How the heck did they get this sofa up here? Or any of this furniture, for that matter?" Yates wondered, looking at the chunky antique desk and captain's chair.

"Beats me," Anna said, tucking her feet up into a cross-legged position. The mannerism bore no resemblance to their preconceived notions of what an academic historian should look like, or how they should behave, and there was not a scrap of tartan or tweed in sight. "All this furniture was here when I arrived. I just added a few of my own bits and bobs."

One such 'bob' was a large, silver-framed portrait photograph of herself and Ryan, taken on their wedding day on the beach at Bamburgh. In days gone by, Melanie might have looked at that photograph with a generous dollop of envy; but now, she smiled and looked across to the man who was fast becoming her own special partner in life.

If he played his cards right, of course.

"So, how can I help?" Anna asked. "You said something about an old symbol being used as a sort of calling card in a spate of hate crimes?"

Jack nodded, and set his cup down to retrieve the small brown folder he'd brought with him. He proceeded to lay out a series of close-up images on Anna's desk, taken from the synagogue and the mosque, showing the same symbol with three interlocking triangles.

Anna leaned forward to study the images.

"The *valknut*," she said, immediately.

"Do you know what it means?" Melanie asked. "I wondered whether it was a Neo-Nazi symbol, but Jack thinks it could be old Nordic."

"Actually, you're both right," Anna said, and walked over to the bookshelf that took up an entire wall of her study. She peered at the titles for a moment, and then tugged one of them from an upper shelf. She flicked through the pages until she came to one with a series of old archaeological photographs, each showing the same carved, interlocking triangles.

"The *valknut* is associated with the Norse god, Odin," she said. "In old Norse mythology, Odin was not only the ruler of all the Norse gods, he was also the god of war and death."

"That sounds ominous," Melanie muttered, and looked at the book Anna showed her.

"In Norse mythology, warriors who lost their lives in battle earned themselves a place in Valhalla, which means 'the hall of the slain'. This grand hall was ruled by Odin, so any warrior who entered would become one of his adopted sons, so the story goes. The *valknut* is an extension of this, meaning 'knot of the slain'."

"Where does the white supremacy bit come in?" Lowerson asked.

"Well, you have to be careful to look at the broader context," Anna cautioned. "Some non-racist, peaceful neo-Paganists use the symbol and call themselves 'Odinists' without any negative connotation. However, there's a supremacist group of Odinists who have appropriated the symbol. That seems to be the case here, in the pictures taken from the synagogue and the mosque."

The other two nodded.

"We need to nip this in the bud, and quickly," Yates said. "With all the stuff going on in the world at the moment, people feel unsettled; and, when they're unsettled, tempers run high. We've worked for a long time to foster a peaceful relationship between the different cultural and religious groups, especially in the west end of Newcastle. The last thing we want is for that balance to be destroyed."

Anna tucked the book back onto the shelf.

"I need to make something clear," she said. "Of all the different symbols that have been used at one time or another to signify racist white or Christian supremacy, the *valknut* is one of the most dangerous. It's generally understood by extremists to mean that they're willing to die on the battlefield, for a cause they believe in. These aren't your garden variety fruitcakes."

The other two nodded.

"Extremist Odinism is spreading," Anna said. "Particularly in America and here in the UK. There's an offshoot of the religion called 'Asatru', which is an Icelandic word meaning 'belief in the gods'. It emphasises the magical elements of early polytheistic religions, such as Odinism. Unfortunately, plenty of white supremacist groups have appropriated Asatru and follow a racist interpretation."

"This is ringing a few bells," Yates said, in worried tones. "Wasn't Anders Breivik an Odinist?"

She referred to the infamous terrorist, who shot dead seventy-seven people in Norway, back in 2011.

"Yeah—Brenton Tarrant, too," Lowerson said. "He killed fifty-one people in Odin's name, in New Zealand, earlier this year."

"There was an internal memo sent around to all academic staff less than a month ago, warning us to be on the lookout for men or women defacing sites of historic, religious or cultural importance," Anna put in. "It followed the defacing of several sites of historic importance all around the country, including the Avebury Stone Circle, down in Salisbury."

"Did they mark the stones with this symbol?" Lowerson asked, tapping a finger on one of the photographs.

"I'm not sure," she said, honestly. "But the leader of the group was telling his followers to be prepared to die in battle, in the name of Odin."

"Jack, I take back what I said earlier," Melanie said, after a lengthy pause. "Religion has a lot to answer for, after all."

CHAPTER 16

The skies over Northumberland were beginning to turn overcast as a blanket of steel-grey clouds moved in from the sea. There was a chill to the air that heralded the coming autumn, and Ryan flicked on the heater inside his car as he and Phillips made their way back along the long 'military road' towards Otterburn.

"We were too late, Frank."

Phillips glanced across at his friend's stern profile, and could see very clearly the sadness and frustration beneath the calm veneer.

"We couldn't have done anything differently," he said. "The Army gave the soldiers a full debrief and there was a counsellor booked in to see them all, this morning."

"She didn't even wait to see if she was right," Ryan said, softly. "Jess Stephenson was so convinced she was responsible, she took her own life."

He turned to his friend with blazing silver-grey eyes.

"Were we too hard, Frank? Was...*I* too hard on her?"

"Nay, lad," Phillips said, and put a comforting hand on his shoulder. "You did your duty, and you did it fairly. Nobody could say otherwise."

Ryan was silent for the rest of the journey but, as the car moved through the main security gates, he made up his mind about something.

"I'm officially opening a murder enquiry into the death of the unidentified woman," he said, decisively. "I want a Major Incident

Room set up here, on-site, where everybody can see us and, more importantly, where we can see them."

"Aye, that Winchester hunting bullet seems fishy to me."

"I don't know whether it's fishy, but it's certainly unexplained, and I have a lifelong aversion to unexplained things."

"Po-tay-to, po-tah-to," Phillips said. "But Morrison won't like you setting up the MIR away from Police HQ. Only last week, she was on about us sticking to our desks rather than scampering about the countryside."

"I don't tend to do much 'scampering', as a rule," Ryan drawled. "But the day I'm chained to a desk is the day I die."

"Amen to that," Phillips said. "Howay and let's go catch a killer."

"Couldn't have put it better myself."

* * *

Faulkner's team of CSIs had already arrived at the scene, by the time Ryan and Phillips made their way back out to Witch Crags. This time, they made for a small woodland area nearby, where Private Jess Stephenson had apparently decided to end her days.

Much as it grieved him, Ryan had given orders that, as it was clear no life-saving resuscitation could be performed, she was to remain where she was until the CSIs could photograph the area and take full swabs before the surroundings were contaminated by outside forces.

Once that process was complete, Ryan cut her down himself.

It was a thankless task, and the image of Jess Stephenson's horribly bloated and mottled skin would no doubt haunt him for many years to come. However, he handled her body with the utmost care, transferring her onto a waiting stretcher before she was transported to the mortuary and into Jeffrey Pinter's safekeeping.

As the stretcher was lifted away by four soldiers, Ryan looked down at his gloved hands, which still held Stephenson's brown, military-issue leather belt, and the knife he'd used to cut it from her neck. With a last, lingering look at the simple contraption that had taken a life, he slipped the belt into a plastic evidence bag and handed it to Faulkner, who was waiting nearby.

"You didn't have to do that, yourself," the man said. "We'd have brought her down."

"I was glad to help," Ryan replied, and cast his sharp gaze around the vicinity and across to where Phillips was taking statements from the group of army privates from 3rd Platoon, who had been the ones to find Jess a short while ago.

The patch of woodland was small but dense; the pine trees having grown close to one another so their fragrance filled their nostrils, mercifully blotting out the less salubrious scent of death that might otherwise have infused the morning air. The forest floor was thick with discarded cones and smaller branches which crackled beneath their plastic-coated feet and, a short distance away, an army-model quad bike was parked with the keys still swinging in the ignition.

"That must be how she got up here," he surmised, nodding towards the vehicle.

Faulkner followed his gaze and nodded.

"It looks like it," he said. "We'll dust it for prints."

Ryan nodded, and wondered how much to say. It was important that the forensics team were free to complete their duties without any preconceptions or bias, wherever possible; however, if there was a particular line of enquiry, it was equally important to let them know so they could pay attention to the finer details that might be significant.

He decided on a middle road.

"Did you find any shell casings for a .308 calibre Winchester bullet, during your search yesterday?" he asked.

Faulkner frowned, and referred to the preliminary report he'd only recently drafted.

"No, I'm almost certain we found nothing of that kind. We found plenty of smaller calibre shells, more like 5mm, which I anticipate will be a match to the bullets used during the tactical exercise, yesterday. Why do you ask?"

Ryan thought of the kind of distance that could be covered by a long-range hunting rifle, and wondered where the unknown sniper had stationed himself, when he'd fired a single shot at the woman who now lay on a metal slab at the mortuary. The preliminary report from the pathologist indicated that the Winchester bullet had been found lodged in her skull, with a trajectory that suggested the woman was shot from behind, as she was running away.

Bearing in mind where she fell, that put the position of the unknown gunman somewhere to the east, towards Witch Crags. However, Ryan knew that hunting rifles could maintain accuracy over hundreds of metres, and there was every chance the person who fired the Winchester .308 bullet did so from some distance away. They'd have needed high-spec night vision goggles, like the rest of the platoon section, but it was possible.

That knowledge alone was enough to give him pause, because the very idea suggested the existence of a perpetrator who was highly organised, in possession of high-tech equipment and who may, or may not, have been responsible for driving the victim out into a live-fire training exercise.

But why? Ryan thought.

What was the motive?

He took a final look around the little enclave of forest, and thought about Jess Stephenson's family, and of the young woman he'd spoken to less than twenty-four hours ago.

Had there been something else in her eyes that he'd missed?

He, who was so good at reading people and behaviour, had utterly missed the signs that must have been there, plain as day. Why hadn't he seen that Jess Stephenson was close to the edge, and that she was ready to end her own life?

"Ryan—?"

He realised Faulkner was waiting for a response.

"There's a possibility the woman yesterday wasn't hit by an army-issued bullet," he said, quietly. "Pinter found a Winchester .308 bullet lodged in the woman's skull, but none of the army firers carry that kind of weapon. It isn't even part of their arsenal—I checked."

Faulkner was quick to join the dots.

"You think this hasn't got anything to do with the army, after all?"

Ryan narrowed his eyes and gave a brief nod.

"I'm beginning to think we've been looking at this from the wrong direction, all along."

CHAPTER 17

"How about fish and chips for lunch?"

MacKenzie's suggestion was met with an eager affirmative from Samantha, and the pair of them made their way along to the high street in Wooler, where a small, traditionally-styled fish and chip van tended to park itself, in time for the lunchtime crowd.

Fishy on a Dishy was another triumph of Northern brand-marketing, MacKenzie thought, as they joined the small queue, and she found herself humming the old folk tune beneath her breath.

"Thou shalt have a fishy, on a little dishy...thou shalt have a fishy, when the boat comes in...dance to thy daddy, sing ti' thy mammy..."

'What are you singing?" Samantha asked.

"It's a traditional Northumbrian song," MacKenzie said. "Every part of the world has its own traditions and customs, folk songs and whatnot."

"Do they have it in Ireland, where you're from?"

MacKenzie nodded.

"They've got different songs, there," she said, and felt a sudden pang of homesickness, something she hadn't felt for a long time.

"What'll it be, ladies?"

The man behind the counter was so large, he seemed to fill the whole van. He was around forty, tall and very muscular beneath the traditional white fishmonger's outfit he wore, and looked as though he'd be more at home in a boxing ring than a fish and chip van.

"Um, we'll have a large cod and chips, and a small portion of scampi, please."

"Comin' right up," he said, and the pair watched as he trowelled a generous portion of cholesterol-laden chips into a takeaway box. "Haven't seen you for a couple of days," he added, as he bustled around getting their order together. "Been having plenty of fun, over at the holiday camp?"

Samantha nodded eagerly.

"Yeah! There's loads of stuff to do there, but I like the swimming pool the best," she said.

MacKenzie smiled and handed over the money to pay, but when he reached over to take the cash from her, his fingers brushed against hers in a manner too practised to be accidental. Surprised by the unexpected contact, she snatched her fingers away and found him smiling at her with laughter in his eyes.

"Have a nice day, bonny lass."

MacKenzie gave him a long, level look, and then deliberately turned away.

But, when she glanced back, she found him watching her with a fixed intensity she found unnerving.

"Come on, Sam," she murmured. "Let's go back."

* * *

After their meeting with Anna, Jack kept his promise to Melanie and they went for a lunchtime stroll along the river in Durham, stopping off for some provisions on the way. He would have liked to stay much longer, whiling away the hours on the riverbank with a beautiful woman by his side, but there was work to be done and all the talk of extreme Odinism was deeply unsettling.

Matters did not improve when, almost as soon as they were back on the road to Police Headquarters, Jack received another call from the Control Room.

This time, the target had been a successful black footballer for the local premiership team, whose home had been letter-bombed in a style similar to the attack on the Central Mosque, the day before.

"That's two in as many days, which means they're escalating quickly," Jack said. "We need to consult with Ryan on the best approach, and have a word with GCHQ to see if they have anything on their radar that can help us."

Melanie nodded.

"I can't imagine how terrifying that would be, waking up to find an explosion in your own home."

Jack nodded.

"It's lucky that nobody was home. The family are away on holiday, apparently, so the fire only caused property damage."

"Do you think they knew he was away from home?" Melanie wondered. "If Anna's right, and the group we're looking for aren't afraid to die to secure an eternal place at the table in Valhalla, why would it matter to them if he was at home or not?"

"True," Lowerson admitted. "On the other hand, thinking of the psychology behind these groups, it strikes me that most of the people perpetrating these offences are cowards. They don't use normal modes of communication to express any dissatisfaction with politics, or the system, or whatever it is they have a problem with. They turn to hate crime, and mythology. They've had three opportunities to cause grievous bodily harm, or even commit murder, but they haven't gone that far. That means they might talk a good game but, when it comes down to it, maybe they're not ready to have murder on their conscience."

"It's encouraging to think they might have one," Melanie said, and pressed the accelerator to the floor so they practically flew up the A1 dual carriageway back towards Newcastle.

* * *

The dog was back.

He'd worried about the stupid mutt all through the night and, now that it was back, he was unreasonably angry.

He didn't *want* to worry about anyone, or anything.

Never again.

Never again would he care too much about another living thing; it was only a recipe for heartache, and loneliness.

Deliberately, he collected up his meagre possessions and walked away from the dog's uncomprehending face, determined to find himself a new patch.

But, when he looked back, he found that the dog was following.

"Bugger off," he snarled, but the animal wasn't fooled.

There had been no conviction in his voice, and no menace in his heart.

The soldier and the dog stared at one another for an endless moment, and then the dog seemed to tense, its skinny body going on alert.

"What is it?" he asked. "What's the matter?"

When he heard Alfie Rodger's unmistakeable, high-pitched voice echo through the underpass, he knew they'd come for him again, and would keep on coming until he capitulated.

It was only a matter of time.

"Run," he told the dog. "Run, before they see you."

The dog continued to sit there, looking up at him with a trusting expression on its face.

Thinking quickly, he settled himself against the wall and arranged his sleeping bag in a heap beside him, creating a cave of sorts in which the dog could be concealed.

"Here! C'mon, boy. C'mon, that's right," he said, and managed to coax the animal beneath the protective covers of the sleeping bag, just in the nick of time.

CHAPTER 18

Ryan and Phillips set up a makeshift Incident Room in one of the conference rooms at the Otterburn Camp, which was well equipped with telephone lines and printers, should they need them. Ordinarily, Ryan would have taken the time to set up a 'Murder Wall', to provide a visual aid for members of his team to use during the course of their investigation. However, since the conference room door had no lock, he felt it prudent to go without, on this occasion.

The only exception he made was to stick a single photograph on the wall, front and centre, for his team to focus on throughout their discussions. They were a small band, consisting of himself, Phillips, Major Malloy of the Defence AIB, Tom Faulkner, and two crime analysts he'd seconded from his team back at Police Headquarters. Once they were all assembled, he moved to the front of the room and pointed towards the large colour photograph. It depicted a pretty girl of seventeen, dressed in a prom outfit for a high school dance. It had been taken by her parents, four years ago, only weeks before she'd gone missing, never to be seen again.

"This is Layla Bruce," he said, looking across into her smiling, pixelated blue eyes. "She's the woman who died on the ranges yesterday morning. She was twenty-one."

The room became so silent, he could have heard a pin drop.

"A comparison with dental records managed to throw up a match with one of our cold-case 'Missing Persons' files," he explained. "Layla was first reported missing on 1st March 2015 by her parents, who became concerned when she didn't return home from school."

He wondered whether it would give them any comfort to know where she was, now, or whether they would rather have lived with the dreadful, desperate hope that she was still alive, somewhere out there in the world. Unfortunately, the choice would be taken out of their hands, soon enough.

"Layla came from St Boswells, a village on the south side of the River Tweed, just over the border into Scotland."

"All that time, she'd been so near," Phillips said, with a small shake of his head.

"We don't exactly know where she's been, for the past four years. It's possible she travelled around a bit, especially at first. Although we have no criminal records to back this up, the pathologist report indicates that she was sexually active, and the lack of permanent address suggests to me she may have been getting by as a sex worker."

"It would explain the reason why nobody's reported her missing for a second time," Phillips said. "People who live on the other side of the law don't rush to make reports, in case it puts them on our radar."

"Exactly," Ryan agreed. "The lack of oversight means that people—and particularly women—like Layla are very vulnerable individuals, prone to exploitation and attack."

It upset Ryan to know there were probably thousands of people out there without home or family; vulnerable people who had fallen between the cracks of society to become targets for a very specific kind of predator.

He stuck his hands in his back pockets, while he gathered his thoughts.

"Until now, the only thing we knew about Layla was that she was an unwitting casualty in a routine military exercise. The initial pathology report confirms she sustained a fatal gunshot wound to the head. Other than the bullet, there's no mystery surrounding the cause of death."

"Other than the bullet?" Malloy queried.

"Is the reason we're all here," Ryan said. "The bullet recovered from her skull was a .308 Winchester, suitable for use with a long-range hunting rifle. None of the firers during the tactical training exercise were in possession of a rifle of that kind, and they aren't listed as part of the weapons armoury, here at Otterburn."

"We found no shells matching a .308," Faulkner threw in. "The only cartridge shells we found belonged to the 5.56mm bullets issued to the firers before the exercise, and all were present and accounted for."

"So, you believe there's a mystery gunman," Malloy said slowly.

Ryan shook his head.

"I don't believe it," he said. "I *know* it."

"But—why? Why would anyone shoot a woman who was already running into the pathway of a live-fire exercise?" Malloy demanded.

Ryan scanned each of the faces in the room.

"Isn't it obvious?" he said. "They were hunting big game—a human target—and didn't want to be deprived of the kill."

* * *

Ryan's bald statement was met with an astonished silence.

"You think there aren't people like that, out there in the world?" he said. "Ask yourselves, why do people go to Africa and stalk lions, or elephants, then post pictures of themselves online sitting smugly beside the dead carcasses?"

He swallowed revulsion, at the thought.

"It's not so different," he said softly. "Here, we're sitting in an enormous open landscape, filled with tumbledown houses and pele towers, woods and caves. Better yet, hardly anybody comes out here, other than the army, who stick to a schedule that they helpfully post online. If somebody had a mind to, they could put all that information to use, and live out their worst fantasies."

"If there is somebody out there doing that, why would they let the lass run into the line of army fire? If makes no sense, from their point of view," Phillips argued.

"I agree, and it was a stumbling block to my theory," Ryan said. "That is, until I checked with Major Jones, who told me that the planned schedule of live-fire training for Thursday and Friday was altered, late on Wednesday."

"That's true," Malloy said. "I checked all the details of the advance planning stages, as part of the report I'll be submitting to DAIB."

Ryan nodded, then leaned back against the wall and folded his arms.

"It's conceivable that whoever we're looking for didn't check for any recent updates to the scheduling, particularly as things usually run like clockwork around here. It's possible he or she was taken by surprise, too."

"Are you saying what I think you're saying? You reckon we've got a long-term operator on our hands?"

"I think it's a very strong possibility, Frank. Whoever it is knew how to choose the perfect victim, and managed to lure them or entrap them without fear of discovery," Ryan said, ticking things off each of his fingers. "He or she must have a holding cell of some kind; a safe place he takes them to, before he releases them out onto the moors, where he can chase them like a hound. This place is remote, but he'd need somewhere he can be completely confident his quarry won't escape before he's ready."

"They'd need to be mobile," Faulkner said. "Presumably, they'll have already taken the time to stake out places to pick up their quarry."

Ryan nodded.

"Yes, I think they must have it down to a fine art, by now. I don't have any evidence yet, but I'm going to theorise that the person we're looking for has killed numerous times before."

"Do you think they're army personnel?" Malloy asked, and was almost afraid of the answer. In her line of work, she'd met men and women who'd cracked; gone off the boil, or whatever you wanted to call it. She'd seen their vacant, glassy-eyed expressions as they'd described killing a vulnerable woman or child during an active tour, hoping that people such as herself would not think to investigate.

But they did, and she would.

She believed in a code, just as much as Ryan did.

"I don't know the answer to that," he said, honestly. "It's possible they're ex-military, and they know the terrain well."

Malloy paled slightly, thinking of the headlines that would be splashed all over the news, once word got out.

"Earlier today, I started looking back over old Missing Persons reports," Ryan continued. "Experience teaches us that, at the start of their killing careers, serial killers tend to hunt for victims geographically far away from where they live themselves, although still close enough, or familiar enough, to allow them to move freely and make a quick getaway if need be. As they grow in confidence, the geographic circle gets smaller and smaller, until they get so complacent that they snatch victims who live practically on their own doorstep."

"We don't know that we've got a serial on our hands yet," Phillips said.

"No, but when you look at all the factors I've mentioned, it's a solid possibility. Why else kill Layla Bruce in that way? If she was pushing drugs, or got caught up in something bad, organised gangs don't waste their time or energy hunting people over hill and vale. They'd have killed her, execution-style, and dumped the body or buried it somewhere we'd never find it."

Phillips had to admit that was true.

"If someone's been operating for a while, surely they would have come to our attention, by now," Malloy said.

"Not if they're very careful," Ryan said. "In fact, there's no reason they ever would have come to our attention, until they miscalculated the dates of that training exercise. Even then, there was at least a fifty-fifty chance somebody from CID would have come along and written it all off as an accidental death, then shoved the file in a drawer, somewhere. But they made another serious error, which was to shoot Layla using their own rifle, rather than allowing the soldiers to do the work for him. It would have been safer, and smarter, not to use their own bullet."

Outside, the skies finally opened, and rain began to patter gently against the window panes. To Ryan, it represented the beat of a battle drum, and he turned back to face his small army of troops.

"I want a list of all missing persons within a fifty-mile radius of here, going back over the past ten years," he said. "I want another list of all known red-light districts within the same radius, and we'll need to liaise with local police teams to get the most up-to-date information, on that score. We've got a killer who thinks they own the map, so let's make ourselves a new one."

* * *

It was raining.

The woman could hear it, somewhere outside, and the distant *pitter-patter* brought tears to her eyes.

All around her was darkness, an endless black hole of stagnant air that smelled of old faeces and something much, much worse.

It smelled of death.

At first, she had wondered whether this was where all the bad people went, when they died. Had she been so terribly bad in her life, that she deserved to spend an eternity in such a place?

And *he*—the person who'd brought her here—perhaps he was the devil. Maybe he was her punishment for every trick she'd ever turned, every drug she'd ever taken, every time she'd fallen from grace.

She wasn't dead yet, but she knew she would die in that place, and that nobody would mourn her passing. There would be no search party reported on the six o'clock news, nor any tearful messages from the pillars of her community—for she had no community.

She only had herself, which was how it had always been.

She leaned her aching head back against the damp stone wall and listened.

She could still hear the rain.

She must be alive.

CHAPTER 19

The Bruce family lived in a smart bungalow overlooking the golf course in St Boswells—a village in the Scottish Borders known chiefly for being a stopping point along St Cuthbert's Way, which was a sixty-two-mile pilgrimage trail connecting the Scottish town of Melrose and the Holy Island of Lindisfarne, off the coast of Northumberland. Ryan and Phillips made the journey from Otterburn through a steady fall of rain, and then sat for a moment by the kerb with the windscreen wipers *swooshing* back and forth, to gather their strength for the emotional ordeal that lay ahead.

"Never gets any easier, does it?" Ryan murmured.

"Nope," Phillips said, roundly. "Wine gum?"

"No thanks."

They watched the windscreen wipers for another minute or two in companionable silence, while Phillips chomped on his wine gums.

"It scares the hell out of me, when I think about how their girl was only seventeen when she left home, or went missing. That's only seven years older than Samantha is now."

Ryan nodded.

"Not that I have much experience of this first-hand, but I've heard that the main job of a parent is to worry constantly."

Phillips snorted.

"You're not wrong. Sam asked me the other day if she could walk down to the corner shop for a bag of sweets on her own, and I was worried sick. It was just normal, though, when we were kids."

Ryan thought back to his own, highly regimented childhood as the son of a high-ranking British diplomat and thought that there was a time when he would have given all that he owned for the kind of freedom Frank had enjoyed.

"You'll find the right balance, Frank. You and Denise seem to do it as naturally as breathing."

Phillips gave him a startled look.

"I—well, thanks, lad. It doesn't always feel that way."

He paused, wondering whether to ask the next, highly personal question on his mind. Sensing his indecision, Ryan smiled and took pity on him.

"Not yet," he said.

"What?"

"The answer to your question is, 'not yet'," Ryan repeated. "Anna and I are looking forward to being parents, one day, but there isn't any mad rush. Also—"

He hesitated, unsure whether to discuss matters that were so close to the heart. Then again, Frank was more than just his sergeant, or his friend.

He was family.

"The fact is, Frank, we're not sure whether Anna will be able to have children."

Phillips put a hand on his friend's arm in silent support.

"I'm sorry, lad," he said quietly. "It was insensitive of me to ask. I never thought—"

"No, neither did we," Ryan said, and his lips twisted. "Keep your fingers crossed for us."

"Fingers, eyes and toes," Frank promised.

Ryan nodded, and let out the breath he'd been holding.

"Right, shall we get this over with?"

"Howay then," Phillips said, reaching for the door. "Age before beauty."

* * *

Margaret Bruce had the hollow-eyed look of a woman who hadn't slept in four years.

When she answered the door, she looked between the two detectives and clutched a hand to her throat.

They knew, Ryan thought. *Mothers always knew, long before he said the words*

"Mrs Bruce?"

"Stuart!" she called out to her husband, who'd been sitting reading a paper in the living room.

"What is it, love? Who—?"

"Mr and Mrs Bruce?" Ryan held out his warrant card. "I'm DCI Ryan and this is my colleague, DS Frank Phillips. We're from Northumbria CID. May we come in?"

He saw the conflict on the woman's face; the fleeting, hopeless thought that, if she refused them entry, it would delay the rest.

"Come in," her husband said quietly.

Both men stepped inside and wiped their feet on the mat.

"You'd better come through," Stuart Bruce said, as his wife began to cry silently.

Ryan felt a burning at the back of his throat, a tight ball of emotion he kept under rigid control. It was not his place to cry with these people; that wouldn't help them to recover from the loss of their daughter.

Once they were seated on the sofa, Ryan said the words.

"I regret to inform you that your daughter, Layla, was killed yesterday morning. Please accept our sincere condolences for your loss."

The words were trite and formal, but there were no better ones. He'd tried them all.

Margaret's shoulders began to shake violently, and she let out a gut-wrenching sob. From the corner of his eye, Ryan caught the stiffening of his friend's shoulders and knew that Phillips too was fighting his own battle against a rising tide of emotion.

Margaret's husband drew her body towards him and they clung together for long minutes, while Ryan and Phillips waited, feeling horribly voyeuristic.

"How?" she managed to whisper. "How did she die?"

"Our enquiries are ongoing, Mrs Bruce, but your daughter was killed during a night-time, live-fire tactical training exercise at the Otterburn Ranges."

Ryan drew out a hand-written card, signed by all the officers from the 1st Royal Welsh Fusiliers, and left it on the coffee table.

"The Army will be contacting you separately but, in the meantime, they've asked me to convey their deepest sympathies."

"Was she a soldier? Had she become a soldier?"

Ryan looked into her desperate eyes, and wished he could give her something to cling to. He wished he knew how Layla Bruce had spent her days, but he didn't, and it was unlikely now that they ever would.

"No, she wasn't a soldier," he said. "I'm sorry, Mrs Bruce, but we're still in the early stages of our investigation. We understand this is a very difficult time for you, but if you can spare us a few minutes to talk about Layla, that would be enormously helpful to us."

"We haven't seen Layla in four years," her father said, and by the pallor of his skin, he seemed to have aged at least ten years since he first answered the door. "We hardly knew our daughter, anymore, detective."

"I understand you filed a Missing Persons Report, back in March of 2015?" Ryan prompted.

Margaret and Stuart nodded.

"She hadn't come home for three days," her mother explained. "That was the worst it had ever been, and I was beside myself. When I went into her room later, I found one of her backpacks missing, and she'd taken some things away with her. The police said that, because she was over sixteen, there wasn't much they could do."

"I'm sorry to hear that," Ryan murmured, and made a mental note to look up the name of the officer who'd handled their case. "Did Layla have a boyfriend at that time?"

Margaret let out an ugly laugh.

"Oh, aye. About ten of them."

"Was there anyone special, or anyone who concerned her?"

They shook their heads.

"She never told us anything like that," Margaret said. "She was very secretive."

Ryan paused to consider how best to frame his next question.

"Did Layla have access to a computer, or a laptop?"

They shook their heads again.

"Well, I mean, I've got my computer in the study, but she didn't use that much. She did have a phone—you know what kids these days are like."

Ryan and Phillips nodded.

"Do you remember the names of any of her boyfriends?" Ryan asked.

"There was one lad," Margaret said. "He was a sweet thing, used to come around almost every day to help her with her studies."

Once again, Ryan and Phillips maintained a professional front, even if they queried what 'helping with her studies' had actually entailed.

"Do you have his name?"

But Margaret began to weep again, and Ryan knew she would soon reach the point where she no longer heard the questions he was asking.

"Why don't you tell us a bit about when she was little?" Phillips suggested, to change the focus. "What did she like to play with, what were her favourite bands and all that?"

"She was a happy little girl with blonde plaits," her father said, and then brushed tears from his eyes. "I don't know when she started to change. Maybe fourteen, or fifteen? I don't know. I just don't know."

"She liked Westlife, and High School Musical. She had one of those banners, from the movie. It's all still there, in her room," Margaret whispered. "You can go in, if you like."

They thanked her, and followed Stuart along the hallway to a bedroom at the very end, which had been locked.

"She doesn't like anything to be moved around, or changed," he warned them.

"We understand, Mr Bruce. Thank you."

They stepped across the threshold and into a dusty lilac bedroom that had once belonged to a girl in her mid or late teens. There was a single bed with a purple cover, and a pile of young teen fiction books on the bedside table. Dozens of printed photographs had been tacked to the wall, their colours now faded with age, and posters of various pop bands had been stuck to the remaining walls in a haphazard fashion.

Phillips opened the wardrobe door to reveal a rack full of nice clothes and shoes, all carefully washed and pressed. On the shelves, there were trinkets from family holidays at home and abroad; everything from musical boxes to tiny figurines of prancing horses.

"It looks like she had a lovely childhood," Phillips said. "Why would a girl like that leave home?"

"I don't think we're speaking to the right people," Ryan said, and tapped a picture of Layla grinning beside a girl of the same age. On the back, she'd inscribed, 'Me and Tammy at Kielder, June 2014'. There were more photographs of Layla with the same girl, in a variety of settings.

"Aye, she's the best friend," Phillips agreed. "Let's see if we can find out her full name, and where she lives now."

* * *

Tammy Crichton still lived with her parents, only a few streets away from the Bruce household. Ryan and Phillips spent some more time with Layla's family but, when it became clear they needed their own space to grieve, they made a respectful retreat.

Serendipitously, Tammy was the one to answer the door when they knocked on the enormous brass knocker carved in the shape of two giant golf balls.

"Sorry, Pearl isn't home," she said, operating on automatic pilot. Her mother was captain of the ladies' golf team, which made her de facto head of all things gossip-related in the town, and it was a running joke in the Crichton household that they might as well replace the front door with a revolving one.

"We haven't come to see her—we've come to see you, actually. It's Tammy, isn't it?" Ryan asked, and began to fish out his warrant card.

"Oh, my God—oh, my God," she said, in quick succession. "First of all, let me just say, it's ridiculous that Ally would call the police over something so trivial. I've already told her, I'll pay for a new air-con system, for heaven's sake. It wasn't like I broke it on purpose!"

"We're not here to discuss property damage, either," Phillips said, in his best fatherly tone. "We're from Northumbria CID, and we want to talk to you about your old friend, Layla Bruce."

Tammy's face fell.

"Oh. You'd better come in, then."

* * *

Tammy made herself a cup of tea, belatedly offered them one—which they politely declined—and led them through to a sunroom dominated by flowery chintz sun loungers and what seemed to be acres of golfing trophies and other memorabilia.

"Sorry about the junk," she said. "It's all they do."

"They?" Phillips asked.

"My parents," she supplied, with a roll of her heavily-lined eyes.

"Right, well, thank you for your time, Ms Crichton. We understand you were friends with Layla Bruce?"

"*Were*, is right," she said, bitterly. "We used to be tight, but then she got this boyfriend and he was all she could talk about. It was boring."

"You don't happen to remember the name of this boyfriend, do you?"

"Course I do. She wouldn't shut up about him, would she? He was called Pete Caldwell. Said he came from over in Melrose and that he was a photographer for all the actors and pop stars and that."

She huffed out a laugh.

"I can't believe she fell for that. As if some bloke called Pete from Melrose was a celebrity photographer! He probably worked down at the Cash 'n' Carry."

She took a slurp of tea, pleased with herself for that last jibe.

For Ryan's part, he didn't mind how the information came out; just so long as it did.

"So, Melrose Pete," he said, to make her laugh. "What did he look like? Do you know how old he was?"

"Well, I'm going back to 2014, start of 2015, yeah? He was sort of tall, with dark blonde hair a bit darker than Layla's. He had these weird, golden-brown eyes. She used to say they were *mesmerising*," Tammy said, using her fingers to affect quotation marks. "I think he was about twenty-five."

"And she was sixteen?" Phillips queried, his newly-discovered paternal instincts getting the better of him.

"Yeah," Tammy nodded. "Lookin' back, I s'pose it was a bit pervy."

She shuffled in her chair.

"So, what's all this about, anyway? Has she got herself in trouble with the law?"

"Layla was killed, yesterday morning."

Tammy's mouth fell open, into a perfect 'o' of surprise, then her eyes welled with tears.

"Dead? She's *dead*?" Tears spilled over, running tracks through the make-up on her cheeks. "I—look, when I was saying all that stuff before…I didn't mean. We were friends all through school. She was really fun to be around, and we had a laugh. How did she die? Was there an accident?"

Ryan shook his head.

"I'm sorry, I can't talk about any of those details at the moment, but it would be very helpful to our investigation if you could tell us anything important you can remember about Layla, or her boyfriend."

Tammy used the edge of her cuff to wipe away her tears and, by force of habit, Ryan reached into the inner breast pocket of his jacket and brought out a small packet of Kleenex that he reserved for occasions such as these.

"Thanks," she said, and blew her nose loudly.

"Um, well, I know she was having trouble at home," Tammy began. "Maggie and Stu are really nice people, but they're strict. No short skirts, church on Sundays, that kind of thing."

Ryan and Phillips nodded.

"Anyway, Layla just wasn't cut out for the quiet life. She loved to be out, meeting people, laughing, having fun. She didn't want to be stuck at home watching *Antiques Roadshow.*"

Ryan could hardly blame her.

"So, the relationship was strained?"

"Yeah, you could say that. Layla was dabbling in a bit of weed, back then, and her dad hit the roof when he found out. Said she should be focusing on schoolwork, but you've got to understand, she wasn't into it. She just didn't enjoy it."

"So, she left?"

"Yeah, apparently. She never told me, and I guess I never forgave her for that," Tammy admitted. "All these years, when she's been off living it up, I've been stuck here in St Boswells, working at the Golf Club Bar."

Ryan smiled, but it didn't reach his eyes.

"Believe me, Tammy. If your friend could trade places with you, right now, she would. Many other people would, too."

CHAPTER 20

The woman awoke in darkness.

It was so empty, so complete, she thought she had died and been reborn to a half-world, somewhere between heaven and hell. She no longer heard the patter of raindrops somewhere in the outside world, nor the scurry of rats and mice beneath the floorboards at her feet.

She missed them.

She missed having the sunshine on her skin, the wind in her hair.

She missed her mother.

She missed her son.

He didn't know her, of course. They'd taken him away, just as soon as they'd found out what she did, and what she was.

Druggie.

Prostitute.

She was both, and yet she was neither.

Did either of them mean she couldn't love the small, perfect bundle that had been the lasting gift of a man she'd never known? Did they know how hard she'd fought against the symptoms of withdrawal, to keep his little body free of her toxins?

All for nothing—they'd taken him, anyway.

And, as so many people had told her, it was for the best.

For the best, for the best, for the best, her mother said. And, soon enough, she'd said it too. She recited it, like a mantra, every time she looked at herself in the mirror. She told herself not to worry about him, wherever he was now, because he had a family that would love him, and give him all the things she never could.

For the best, for the best, for the best.

Tears ran down her skin and onto her knees, which she pulled up to her chin. She clasped her arms around her legs as half-formed memories swirled around the darkness beside her.

* * *

Lowerson and Yates made their way directly to the large, leafy road in Gosforth where one of its most prominent inhabitants had recently become the latest victim of an Odinist hate attack.

Daniel Odawu was Newcastle United's most recent star acquisition, with pundits saying he had not one but two magic feet, when it came to scoring goals. Naturally, the price of those feet had been eye-wateringly high, but it made the fans happy and the club happy, too. It didn't hurt that Daniel was a family man with a glossy-looking wife and two perfect children; nor did it hurt their opinion polls when people learned that he volunteered regularly at homeless shelters and food banks throughout the city, before returning to his enormous detached home in the city's premier locale.

Though Daniel was British, as was his father and mother, he was of West African descent; a small factor that made no difference whatsoever to his army of loyal fans, but a lot of difference to the extremist minority group who had decided to target his home.

"Bloody hell," Yates said, eloquently.

Even severely fire-damaged, the three-storey mansion Odawu called home was an impressive sight to behold.

"Remind me again, will you? Why did I choose to become a detective, rather than a footballer?" Lowerson asked.

"That would be because you can't play football," Melanie said, helpfully.

"Ah yes, now I remember."

They wandered across to where the Fire Investigator was making notes on a large clipboard, having found a perch on the edge of the ornamental fountain that was the centrepiece of the driveway.

"Careful it doesn't start up, all of a sudden," Melanie said, eyeing the giant marble dolphins with frank suspicion.

The Fire Investigator chuckled.

"Don't worry, I've turned the mains off," she said. "Some of the pipes had burst, thanks to the heat and the pressure, so we just shut it all off once the blaze was in hand."

"Pity about the house," Lowerson said. "But it's a relief nobody was home."

The investigator nodded.

"The letter bomb had a bigger reach, this time," she said. "If anybody had been within twenty yards when it detonated, you'd be talking risk to life."

"It definitely feels as though the attacks are getting worse," Yates remarked. "Would you say the same?"

The investigator nodded.

"The first attack—at least, the first we've attributed to the same group of people—seemed more amateurish, whereas the last two attacks are definitely in another league. The craftsmanship of the incendiary device is quite sophisticated, for example, and I'd say they chose the area to spray-paint their symbol with a bit more care."

"Where'd they choose, this time?" Lowerson asked, and the investigator jerked her head in the direction of the lawned gardens, around the back of the house.

"Come and take a look at this," she said.

They followed her around the side of the mansion, through an intricate iron gate with gold-leaf detailing, and around to the back patio. There, an enormous *valknut* symbol had been mown into the grass.

"Well," Yates said. "They certainly didn't feel like they had to rush, did they?"

"Probably because they managed to deactivate the security system," the investigator said. "It's a complex system, with several indoor and outdoor cameras, linked remotely to the local police station as well as Odawu's own smartphone, so he can turn the alarm off remotely and so on."

"If they managed to deactivate it, they must have a systems expert in their group, or at their disposal," he said. "Either that, or somebody who used to work for the security company."

"There's been quite a crowd, all morning," the investigator said. "A couple of the local bobbies have been keeping them back, but you're bound to get a few paps trying to get over the fence for a look inside the house."

"Odawu's solicitor emailed earlier today, to say he'd engaged a private security firm to assist the police," Lowerson said. "Odawu himself is coming back on the first flight from St Bart's tomorrow."

"What about the components used to make the incendiary device?" Yates asked, and dragged her wayward mind back from thoughts about rum cocktails and sunset walks on a Caribbean beach.

"We're still analysing them," the investigator said, with a note of apology. "The lab's going as fast as it can, but we've had a busy couple of weeks, with one thing and another."

Yates nodded.

"In the meantime, we'll wait to see what the CSIs come back with. Who knows—maybe, one of these morons will have left a fingerprint on the ride-on lawnmower?"

"Maybe Newcastle will win the league?" Lowerson quipped. "We can always live in hope."

CHAPTER 21

The rain stopped suddenly, as though somebody had turned off a tap somewhere in the sky. As the sun broke through the clouds, it cast an enormous rainbow over the county, but it could not displace the spectre of murder and suicide that presently hung over the soldiers encamped at Otterburn.

After speaking to Layla's family and closest friend, Ryan and Phillips gave instructions for urgent enquiries to be made about a Pete Caldwell, living in Melrose. While they waited for further information to come through about Layla Bruce—from her GP, her bank, her telephone provider and the forensics team—they decided to turn their minds to the other, no less important death, which had occurred that very morning.

The atmosphere around the camp was subdued, to say the least. Soldiers kept to their dorms or to themselves, while a search was made of Private Jess Stephenson's bunk area to see if they could find any clue as to her mindset when she'd left the camp, early that morning.

Ryan and Phillips stood a safe distance away from the bunk while Faulkner's team went over the area, their suits rustling as they shuffled around the floor and under the bed.

"I still can't wrap my head around it," Phillips said, in an undertone. "I can't believe she took her own life, believing she'd killed someone in the line of duty."

Ryan made a non-committal sound.

"We haven't had any of the results back from the scene this morning," he said. "I agree, it looks a lot like suicide, but we've seen plenty of those staged before."

"True," Phillips said. "But for what reason?"

"None, that we know of," Ryan said. "But you and I both love a good mystery, don't we?"

"I love a good curry, n'all, but it doesn't mean I'm lookin' for one all the time."

They both came to attention, as did the military personnel in the room, when Lieutenant Colonel Robson appeared in the doorway.

"Oh, at ease, at ease," he said, waving the formalities away in a manner that gave Ryan the strong impression he would be sorely put out if those formalities ever slipped.

"How's the search coming along?" he asked.

"As expected," Ryan said, ever the master of understatement.

Robson held out a book he'd tucked beneath his arm. It was a dog-eared copy of *Tinker, Tailor, Soldier Spy*.

"I think I mentioned I was reading this, the other day? Well, I thought I'd better tell you, the book belonged to Private Stephenson, who kindly loaned me her copy before she died. I thought you'd want to have it back."

He held out the book, which Ryan took between a gloved thumb and forefinger.

"Thank you, sir."

"How did it go with the family?" Robson asked. "The Army will, of course, settle all funeral and other bills associated with the woman's burial. Please let us know, when the time comes."

"It's good of you," Ryan said. "But really, that's a decision for the family to make."

"Of course, of course," Robson said. "I quite agree."

They looked across to where Faulkner was beginning to peel back the layers of bedclothes on Private Stephenson's bunk.

"We're all very, very sorry she felt she was left with no other choice, especially given what we now know about the presence of an outside gunman."

Ryan nodded.

"We plan to re-interview everybody over the coming days," he said. "In the meantime, it would be helpful for you to compile a list of all soldiers—including those permanently stationed here at Otterburn—who have a licensed or unlicensed hunting rifle, .308 calibre. The sooner we have those names, the sooner we can start to eliminate them."

A shadow passed over Robson's face, but he nodded.

"I can't believe any of my officers would be capable of hunting that woman, as if it were a sport," he said softly. "But I'll do as you ask, chief inspector."

"Thank you. If you could also ask them to think back and make a note of any times or dates when they may have witnessed anyone carrying a hunting rifle of that kind, that would also save us some valuable time."

"Certainly, chief inspector."

After the CO had departed the room, Ryan looked down at the book he held in his gloved hands and idly flipped through the pages. Private Stephenson had been a doodler, it seemed. Notes had been made in the margins, and what appeared to be a list of numbers—some tens, some hundreds—he assumed to be a totting up of her personal accounts, or something similar.

"Anything interesting?" Phillips enquired.

"I don't think so," Ryan said.

He slid the book inside a plastic evidence bag and added it to the pile of other personal effects Private Stephenson would no longer need.

* * *

The services of a Police Dogs Unit had been requested, in an effort to retrace the path Layla Bruce had taken before she met with her untimely end near Witch Crags the previous day. The pathologist had provided a sample item of her clothing to give the dogs her scent, and Ryan watched them set off across the moors in two small jeeps, the dogs yapping happily as they went.

He turned away from the window and back to the other people in the room, consisting of Phillips, Malloy, and Corporal Amanda Huxley, who had been the first to find the body of Private Stephenson earlier that day.

"Thanks for your time, Corporal," Ryan began. "I know it's been a difficult day."

"Jess was a good soldier, and a good friend," Huxley said, with a catch to her voice. "She'll be greatly missed."

He nodded, and pulled up a chair beside her.

"I'm going to ask you to talk me through what happened when you found Private Stephenson this morning, which might be hard. If you need a break, just let me know."

Huxley nodded.

"I'm alright," she said, with the kind of stoicism he would have expected of one of Her Majesty's finest.

"In that case, can you tell me when you first became aware that Private Stephenson was missing?"

"That would have been shortly after nine o'clock in the morning," Huxley said. "I share a room with Sergeant Major Davies, and she received a message from two female members of her platoon— Privates Becky Grainger and Sarah Abbott—who informed her that their roommate was missing. I happened to be there at the time, so I assisted the sergeant major in raising the alarm."

"I see. And, when was the last time you saw Private Stephenson, personally?"

Huxley thought carefully.

"It would have been in the ladies' bathroom, at around eight o'clock last night," she said. "I thought I heard Jess talking to herself, while I was in the cubicle, but it stopped when I came out. She wished me 'goodnight' and went back to her own dormitory."

"So, you were not altogether surprised to know that Private Stephenson was suffering a mental health crisis, of some form?"

"No, I wasn't surprised," she said. "I booked the counsellor for today, because it's the first appointment they had. I tried to debrief all the trainees about what they'd seen the night before, but clearly I failed to recognise Private Stephenson was in need of more specialist care."

"I'm sure you did all you could," Phillips put in, and she gave him a watery smile.

"How long had you known Private Stephenson?"

"Well, I've been with the 1st Royal Welsh for the past five years, and Jess came to us about a year ago," she replied.

"How did you find her progress, and her aptitude for the job?"

"Both excellent," she said, without a pause. "I'd have tipped Jess Stephenson for officer candidacy in the next twelve to eighteen months."

"Did she speak to you about her feelings or emotions following the tactical exercise, yesterday?"

Huxley lifted a shoulder.

"She only spoke when spoken to," she explained. "For an infantry soldier, that's an exemplary quality… but, for a human being, it can be antisocial. The other members of her section felt able to talk about the emotions they were experiencing after learning a woman had died, whereas Private Stephenson remained largely closed off."

Huxley paused, before adding, "She did mention several times that she needed to 'check' something. I don't know what that something was, but, given where she was found this morning, I presume she meant she needed to check back over the incident site yesterday. It breaks my heart to think that, if she'd only waited a few more hours, she would have had the reassurance of knowing she hadn't shot that woman at all; none of our soldiers did."

But Ryan had not ruled out that possibility. It may not have been one of the six firers participating in the tactical exercise, but there was no reason another soldier from the base could not have been on the ranges that night.

"The CO will be compiling a list of all persons licensed to have possession of a personal hunting rifle, in addition to their standard-issue assault rifle, but can I ask you—do you, or do you know of anyone, who owns a hunting rifle with a .306 calibre?"

Huxley moistened her lips, and her eyes darted briefly away, then back again.

"None that I know of."

CHAPTER 22

There was a rainbow over the city of Newcastle upon Tyne, and as the soldier stood by the banks of the river looking up at it, he wondered if it was a sign. A rucksack with all his worldly possessions lay by his feet and, as the office workers began to stream out of the smart, renovated old buildings lining the Quayside, he wondered whether the time had come to bid the world a fond farewell.

He was tired, you see. So tired of waking up each day with a hungry belly and without hope for the future, relying on the charity and disdain of others. So tired of going to sleep at night, wondering if he would even wake up at all.

Once, he'd been a man to be reckoned with but, thanks to the fire, partial blindness had left him unable to use a screen for long periods of time, in an age where computers, laptops, tablets, smartphones and every other kind of phone were king. Ongoing weakness in his hands, arms and legs left him unable to do many types of manual labour without special provision, which some workplaces were unwilling to arrange—not if they could hire somebody else, who needed no such provision. It made it hard for him to type, too, and e-mails at the twenty-four-hour internet café were achieved with slow concentration; not the fast, speed-typing that many office places looked for.

Most of all, there was the crippling PTSD that could strike at any time, reducing him to a shaking, vomiting mess of a man that made others feel uncomfortable to be around.

And still, he tried.

He went along to the internet café every day and searched the database for a job he might be able to do, steeling himself to find an inbox full of rejections from his previous day's efforts. Sometimes, he went along to the People's Kitchen, to remind himself that there were still good people in the world. Other times, he came here, to the river.

And wondered whether it was time to call it a day.

Just then, he felt a nudge against his leg and looked down to find the dog sitting beside him, tail wagging against the pavement as it stared up at him with its dumb, trusting face.

The soldier sighed, and bent down to ruffle its ears.

"What do you call him?"

He turned in surprise to find an old woman standing beside him. She appeared to be out walking a chocolate Labrador that was at least half her size, and looked as though it might make a bolt for the nearest *Greggs* at any moment.

"This here's Charlie," she said, patting the dog's head with a bony hand. "What did you say your dog's called?"

He hadn't.

The soldier looked down at the dog and smiled.

"Naseem," he whispered. "This is my dog, Naseem."

* * *

Ryan and Phillips found Sergeant Major Gwen Davies in the gymnasium, where she was completing a long run on the treadmill. When she spotted them in the doorway, she stopped the running cycle and turned off the music that was blasting from speakers around the room.

"Sorry I'm a bit sweaty," she said, self-consciously. "I could run and have a shower?"

"We don't mind if you don't," Ryan said, with a smile. "We only want to ask a few more questions, in light of events earlier today."

Davies nodded, and took a long swig of water from a bottle emblazoned with the motto, 'STRONGER, HARDER, FASTER'.

"We understand you were the first point of contact, when Privates Becky Grainger and Sarah Abbott contacted you to report their roommate missing. Is that correct?"

Davies nodded, as she wiped sweat from her brow.

"Yes, that's absolutely correct."

"What time was that?" Ryan asked.

"It would have been just after nine," she said. "I happened to be in my room, which I share with Corporal Huxley, at the time."

"What was your reaction, when you heard Private Stephenson was missing?"

Davies raised a hand, then let it fall away again.

"To be perfectly honest with you, chief inspector, I was dubious, at first. Private Grainger is prone to exaggeration, at times, and I wanted to be sure we'd checked all the obvious places before raising a hue and cry. I asked 2nd Lieutenant Dalgliesh to help myself and Corporal Huxley to search the main areas. When, after ten or fifteen minutes of searching, it became clear Private Stephenson wasn't on-base, and hadn't been seen since the previous evening, I felt it wise to inform the CO and convene a full-scale search party."

"Were you surprised that Private Stephenson had gone missing?" Phillips asked.

Davies shook her head.

"No, I can't say I was surprised. She seemed very unsettled after the events on the training exercise, and she believed herself to be wholly or partly responsible. Whilst she took part in the debriefing exercises, she didn't appear to feel any better about the situation following their completion. I had, in fact, registered my concern over her wellbeing with the Medical Officer following the debrief."

Ryan nodded.

"Were you close to Private Stephenson?" he asked. "Despite the difference in rank, would you have considered her a friend?"

"We're all friends in the 1st Royal Welsh, chief inspector."

He nodded towards her wrist, which bore a small support bandage.

"Hurt yourself?"

She looked down at it and pulled a face.

"Nothing specific, just repetitive strain, unfortunately. It's my trigger arm and my writing arm, so it gets the most use."

"That's like me and my tennis elbow," Phillips put in, and Ryan turned to him as though he'd sprouted three heads.

"What?" Phillips said. "They used to call me Frank Sampras, down at the tennis courts."

CHAPTER 23

It was shortly after five when Ryan and Phillips completed the process of re-interviewing the officers at Otterburn Camp, following which they responded to the urgent summons of their Chief Constable and made their way through rush-hour traffic back to Police Headquarters.

Sandra Morrison considered herself a fair woman in most things. She was prepared to accommodate a certain measure of 'charming eccentricity', if and when it brought results. However, there were limits to her patience and, in the light of a forthcoming Commissioner review, she needed to be sure that the men and women under her command were, in fact, under her command.

"Well, if it isn't the prodigal detective," she declared, when Ryan stepped into her office, with Phillips at his heels.

They stood to attention and prepared themselves for what promised to be a dressing down for the memory books.

Morrison eyed the two men in front of her in a mixture of pride and frustration. Though they couldn't be more physically different—and nor could their ages or backgrounds—their personal attributes were remarkably similar and probably explained why they got along so well.

"Ryan, I thought we agreed that, in future, you'd spend less time scampering—what? Is something funny?"

Both men had grinned at the mention of 'scampering', and then rearranged their faces back into neutral.

"Nothing, ma'am."

"Just something in my eye, ma'am."

Her eyes narrowed.

"As I was saying, there'll be no more charging around the countryside—well? What is it now?"

"With respect ma'am, I believe you said 'scampering' rather than 'charging'."

She threw her hands up in the air.

"What difference does *that* make?"

"Oh, there's a great deal of difference between a scamper and a charge," Phillips said, gravely.

Her lips twitched, and she fought valiantly to contain the laugh that bubbled to the surface.

"I—now, look—whether you're scampering, charging, or bulldozing your way around this glorious county, I need you to remember something. This goes for the pair of you," she added. "You have duties and responsibilities here, too. I need to know I can rely on you to manage the staff in your command."

Ryan raised a single eyebrow.

"Has there been any suggestion to the contrary?"

Damn him, she thought, for calling her bluff.

"Well, for starters, can you tell me what progress has been made in the hate crimes case that Lowerson and Yates are running?"

"Certainly," Ryan said, having already sought an update from Lowerson on his way back to the office, as well as a speedy lesson in Nordic symbology from his wife. "DC Lowerson and DC Yates sought expert consultation on the meaning of the symbol that was left at all three of the recent attacks. They learned that it's an old Norse symbol, ma'am, associated with the Viking god, Odin. There's a peaceful branch of the Odinist faith that celebrates all things mystical, but there's a less peaceful, extremist branch that has cropped up in recent years. It's commonly associated with white supremacy groups, and they advocate fighting for their beliefs—until the death. These extremists actively encourage the persecution of those whose beliefs, values or culture differ from their own."

He paused to take a breath, and Morrison gave him a slow clap.

"Alright, you've proved you know all about the symbolism," she said. "What advice did you give your younger colleagues about tracking down these extremists, before any further damage is done? I need hardly remind you, Ryan, it takes very little for tension to build between the communities."

"Indeed, which is why I've advised Lowerson and Yates to focus on legwork," Ryan said. "Knowing the symbolic pretext behind why somebody commits an act of terror doesn't necessarily help you to find and combat the source. Therefore, I've asked them to seek out all available CCTV footage from the main roads and businesses surrounding all three buildings for analysis, dating back over the past two weeks; to have the incendiary devices fully tested and analysed; and to liaise with colleagues in Anti-Terrorism to access shared intelligence that could throw up some potential suspects. I've also asked them to interview and re-interview potential witnesses and look at previous offenders with affiliations of this kind who've recently been released from prison."

Morrison was relieved.

"I'm glad to hear it," she said. "Have you considered that this Odinist group may also be responsible for the hunting and execution of the sex worker at Otterburn—Layla Bruce, was it?"

Ryan's ears perked up.

"I hadn't considered that possibility, but it would be in keeping with the ideology of the group, to hunt and persecute those they perceive to be 'undesirable' in the community. However, it would be a side-step from the group's usual MO, which is to set fire to buildings whilst they are uninhabited."

"Could be a lone wolf," Phillips suggested. "Someone who's part of the group and supports its ideology, but likes his own little projects, too?"

The other two nodded.

"We'll bear it in mind, until further evidence comes to light," Ryan said. "The main problem is trying to build up a picture of Layla Bruce's last movements. She'd had no contact with her family or friends for quite some time and canvassing for witnesses in the local area hasn't turned up anything useful. It might be time to run a *Crimestoppers* campaign, to see if any of her newer friends would be brave enough to get in touch."

Morrison could see the sense in it.

"I'm happy to authorise that," she said. "What else do you need?"

The two men exchanged a glance and wondered if it would be too much to ask for an all-expenses-paid week in the South Pacific.

Perhaps another time.

"I could use a small boost in resources, to pay for an express forensic analysis of the samples taken from the site around where Private Jessica Stephenson's body was discovered earlier today."

She paused.

"Done."

"Th—"

"However," she overrode his next demand. "I expect you to do something in return."

Both men took an involuntary step backwards, and she rolled her eyes.

"The media liaison wants a press conference," she said. "With news leaking out about there being some sort of hunter-killer running amok over the hills, together with the terror attacks in the city, we need to come out with a show of strength."

Ryan could almost feel the sweat breaking out in the base of his spine.

"When?" he asked simply.

She checked her watch.

"About half an hour," she said, and gave him a broad smile. "The local news channels are coming over, and we're both going to speak to them."

Phillips glanced at his friend's crestfallen face, and worked hard to keep his own from cracking up.

"Don't think you're off the hook, Frank. I'll think up something for you, yet."

"Thank you, ma'am," he said, meekly.

CHAPTER 24

As Ryan prepared to stand in front of a roomful of journalists, the woman prowled the walls of her underground cell, trying to work out its dimensions. She counted her footsteps as she crossed from one side to the other, careful to avoid any trip hazards *he* might have left for her to discover, like the tiny razor blades and nails concreted into the walls.

The room was still completely dark.

She counted fifteen footsteps in one direction, and twelve in the other.

Next, she stood completely still and listened. She even closed her eyes, though it made little difference to the light in the room.

At first, all she could hear was her own fast breathing while her body struggled to stay calm, having been in a constant state of 'fight or flight' for more than twenty-four hours. She knew it must have been that long, because she'd started to feel an even greater sense of dread over the past hour or two, and she realised her body's natural rhythms must have been telling her it was almost night-time.

And this hunter preferred to do his hunting at night.

She tried to settle her mind, listening to the surrounding darkness, blocking out everything except the noise in the room.

She heard the scrabbling sound of an insect or a rodent somewhere to her left, and the distant *baa* of a sheep somewhere outside.

Then, she heard it.

The rumbling sound of an engine approaching.

* * *

Having made a swift costume change into a pristine navy suit, Ryan found himself seated at a table beside the Chief Constable, all decked out like a Christmas turkey. Behind them, a large 'exhibition stand' displayed the constabulary crest and logo and, in front of them, there was a row of television cameras and microphones.

"Crack a smile," Morrison said, under her breath.

"If I smile, my face might crack," Ryan shot back. "Besides, you never said smiling was part of the deal."

She gave him a withering look.

"You're a surly, misanthropic git, aren't you, Ryan?" she said, rhetorically. "I have no idea why I like you so much."

That did make him smile, just as she'd hoped.

The cameras started to roll.

"Ladies and gentlemen of the press, I want to thank you for coming to our briefing," she said. "I know I speak not only on behalf of colleagues at the Northumbria Police Constabulary, but on behalf of the entire city, when I say that we are deeply saddened by the recent terror attacks. We pride ourselves on being a warm and generous community here in the North East, and I know many people will be horrified by the dangerous actions of a small minority who do *not* speak for the wider community."

She paused, to let that settle in.

"Many of you will, by now, have also seen the news reports surrounding the death of a woman who has been identified as Layla Bruce, of St Boswells in Scotland. Her next of kin have been informed and I'd like to extend my heartfelt sympathies to them, at this terribly difficult time."

She was good, Ryan thought. There was nothing he disliked more than the public-facing part of his job—which was probably why he'd turned down a promotion to Detective Chief Superintendent on more than one occasion. However, Sandra Morrison was a virtuoso.

"—I'm now going to hand you over to Detective Chief Inspector Ryan."

He came to attention and sat up a little straighter in his seat, focusing on the camera straight ahead of him.

"Thank you," he said. "I'll welcome questions at the end but, before then, I'd like to echo the Chief Constable by offering my sympathies to all those affected by the recent attacks. No matter which faith you follow—or if you follow no religion—we are all equal citizens, whose customs and beliefs are worthy of respect. One of the greatest attributes of our society is the value it places upon individual liberty; that includes the freedom to follow any religion, or to wear any clothing, so long as no harm is done to others. Newcastle Central Mosque is a peaceful place of worship, as is the Synagogue in Gateshead. Those who enter their walls and follow their customs should be able to do so without fear of persecution or attack."

There was utter silence in the room, but for the occasional scribble of pencil on paper.

"The same respect should be afforded to all citizens, regardless of the colour of their skin," he said. "The attack on Daniel Odawu's family home, here in Newcastle, was a shameful one that could have cost lives. I utterly condemn these aggravated hate crimes, and I know my team in the Major Crimes Unit has been working closely with our colleagues in Anti-Terror, and in GCHQ, to apprehend the person or persons responsible."

He reached for a laminated image depicting the *valknut* and held it up.

"On your screens at home, you should be seeing a symbol. This symbol, which is often associated with the white supremacist branch of Odinism, was left at all three of the recent attacks."

Ryan set the picture down again, and looked straight down the camera lens.

"I'm speaking to that group directly, now. If you were responsible for some, or all of these attacks, I ask you to claim them, before somebody else does."

It was important to flush them out, Ryan thought, *however he could.*

"I also say to them, never for a moment believe we won't find you. We will. Never think your deeds will go unpunished because, when I or one of my colleagues uncovers whichever stone you've made your home, we will be seeking to prosecute with the full force of the law."

His tone had been hard and implacable, but now he made it conciliatory.

"However," he said. "There may be one of you out there who is feeling uncertain, or worried that things have gone too far. If you come forward now and give evidence, we can protect you from harm. You can call 111, or the Incident Room number appearing on your screen now."

Ryan ignored the flurry of questions and held up a hand to stave them off.

"Finally, to those of you watching or listening at home, I advise you to be vigilant. Particularly to those belonging to a racial, ethnic or religious minority, I ask you to please be aware of others around you, especially when travelling alone or to places of worship. If you notice anything suspicious, call the emergency number which is 999, the non-emergency police number which is 111, or the Incident Room."

He repeated that number too.

"Turning now to the incident at Otterburn Ranges, I know that all those associated with the army encampment join me in extending their deepest sympathies to the family of Layla Bruce, who was killed in the early hours of yesterday morning during the course of a routine training exercise. Whilst our enquiries remain ongoing, I can confirm that *none* of the firers who participated in that exercise was responsible for her death."

He heard the rumblings of confusion and shock amongst the gathered crowd, followed inevitably by the thrill of a new and vastly more exciting story.

"Chief Inspector—"

"DCI Ryan—"

He ignored the flurry of questions, determined to finish what he had to say.

"On your screen is a picture of twenty-one-year-old Layla Bruce. She was a vulnerable person, who was reported missing by her family in early 2015. We'd like to know more about Layla, and about her life after the time she left home in St Boswells. If you're watching this, or listening to this, and think you knew Layla, please come forward. You can speak to us confidentially, anonymously, and at any time of day. Thank you."

A tidal wave of reporters surged forward, and he barely held back his frustration.

"One at a time, please," he said, and pointed to the first hand he saw, waving frantically at him from the front.

"DCI Ryan! Is it true that one of the soldiers at Otterburn Camp committed suicide, earlier today?"

Ryan swore inwardly. Private Stephenson's family had requested confidentiality for as long as possible, and he also would have preferred a little longer than a few hours to complete enquiries, without the press sniffing around to sensationalise matters.

"A soldier lost their life earlier this morning, in an apparent suicide," Ryan was forced to confirm. "Any further comment would prejudice the ongoing investigation."

"Is the suicide linked to the death of Layla Bruce? Did the soldier murder Layla Bruce?" somebody called out. "Is that why no other arrests have been made?"

Despite best efforts, they could never prevent the leak of information such as this, nor the conclusions people would draw.

"No comment," he said, firmly.

His eye caught on a reflection of the blown-up image of Layla Bruce in a camera lens, which was hanging on one of the exhibition stands behind him, and he thought of the person who had robbed her of life. Was it a crusade-killer, on some holy mission, or was it your bog-standard psychopath, incapable of feeling any remorse?

Ryan leaned forward, and spoke to that person now.

"To the person who killed Layla Bruce, I want you to know something," he said, and the tone of his voice compelled the baying crowd to listen. "There isn't anywhere far enough, or dark enough, for you to hide. You think you know these hills? These are *our* hills, too. Northumberland isn't a hunting ground, and its people aren't your prey."

There was an infinitesimal pause, before he made a promise.

"In case it isn't obvious, the shoe's on the other foot, now. You aren't the hunter, anymore. You're the prey. *My* prey. That is all."

CHAPTER 25

He listened to the press conference on the local radio, from the inside of his van.

You're the prey, the detective said. *My prey.*

He caught sight of himself in the rear-view mirror and wondered, idly, whether he would have been better off dying in Iraq. Perhaps it would have been a kindness to eradicate the sickness; to eliminate the thread of dishonour he'd brought to the uniform and to Her Majesty.

He'd liked it, you see.

The killing.

It's what had first attracted him to the profession, years ago, but it wasn't the kind of answer recruiters liked to hear. *I like to kill people* wasn't high on their checklist of attributes to look for in a soldier.

To his credit, at least he had channelled his impulses. There might be sickness, but there was also logic, and reason. He chose his victims with care, and with precision, and limited himself to what he considered to be 'undesirable' members of society.

Take the creature presently trying to work her way out of the basement room, in the old pele tower he'd bought years ago. She'd be frantic, by now, just as the others had been. It would have been easy to kill her, there at the back of the service station, but where was the lesson in that? She spent her days stuffing heroin in her veins, and she opened her legs to pay for it all.

Was her freedom what he had fought for?

He shook his head, disgustedly.

At least he would give her a sporting chance.

So long as she could run, of course.

* * *

The woman's breath was coming out in pants, now, as she stumbled around the darkened room.

"Help! Please, help!"

She clamped a hand over her own mouth, remembering that the engine she had heard was more likely to be him, not some kind stranger come to rescue her.

Oh, God.

Please, God. Help me.

Her hands splayed on the wall and she tried once again to find a window, or a hidden door…anything she could use to escape. At first, there was only damp stone, but then she felt the sharp nick of a razor, and the scratch of nails. She cried out, snatching her hand away.

Then, a thought struck.

The razors hadn't been stuck all over the walls—only in one concentrated area, on the back wall.

Perhaps, as a deterrent to curious hands.

She licked her lips and placed her hands on the wall again, this time with extreme care. Her fingers tapped it, as if the wall were braille, moving in lines up and down. She was starting to lose hope, when her fingertips connected, not with the sharp end of some metal, but with something raw and wooden at about the same height as her head.

She risked placing her hands against it, and pushed slightly, hearing the give of a hinge at the top.

It was a window, she realised. *Boarded up with plyboard, and painted many times in black.*

Elation gave way to crippling fear, when she heard the sound of a car door slamming outside.

Shortly after, there came the soft tread of footsteps on the floorboards above her.

One, two, three…fifteen.

He'd stopped, directly above her head.

CHAPTER 26

The soldier and his dog made their way back to the underpass, bellies full of homemade chicken broth and bread. There'd been a big line at the kitchen, that night—the biggest he'd ever seen. It was the same at the shelter, too, and he'd known just by looking at it that he didn't stand a chance, even though he'd saved the money all week to sleep in a proper bed.

When he'd been a younger man with a home of his own, he remembered wondering what kind of person ended up on the streets.

Couldn't they get a job?

Couldn't they sort themselves out?

He'd asked those questions, and more. He'd walked past men like him, along the same underpass, wearing his best togs—like the young philosopher the day before. He'd probably had a girl on his arm, too, but he hadn't bothered to stop or ask any names. He'd probably turned away to stare intently at the floor, as most people did when they passed him now.

He found his usual patch, which was blessedly clear of any usurpers or suspicious-looking yellow puddles and began to make their bed for the night. He had some fresh cardboard, which he laid out first, and then huddled into his sleeping bag. The lass down at the shelter hadn't had a room for him, but she'd run the bag through the wash, so it smelled like lavender.

Nice kid, he thought. She didn't have to do that.

He looked up and down both sides of the underpass, along its shadowed concrete tunnels, and leaned his head back against the wall.

The dog settled himself against his hip, resting its wolfish snout against his thigh, and looked up at him, as if to say, "Well?"

"Bossy," he muttered, but obliged the mutt with a long scratch between the ears. "There. Is that better?"

If dogs could smile, this one did.

* * *

She began to tremble, and she stood still, her body frozen in fear.

The footsteps had stopped somewhere above her head, as if he already knew where she was. A fatalistic sense of doom washed over her, as her body slowly began to shut down, accepting the inevitable.

There was nobody to miss her.

Nobody to care.

For the best, for the best, for the best.

But then, something happened. Some forgotten part of herself cried out, a primal scream to remind her that her life was precious. Just as precious as anybody else's.

She spun around to the wall and pressed her hands against the small wooden rectangle above her head and began tracing her fingers over the edges to search for an opening, or a hinge. The nails and razors caught her skin until the warm blood ran over her wrists, but she gritted her teeth and bore down.

Above her head, the footsteps moved again, and she let out a small, whimpering sound of panic.

He was coming for her.

* * *

They'd come for him, again.

Alfie Rodgers had brought reinforcements, this time, and the soldier knew his thinking time had come to an end.

"Hello, mate! Nice to see you!"

Alfie was flanked by three heavy-set men of different ages, but each of them had the cold, dead eyes of a shark. He looked this way and that, but the underpass had grown quiet, now that most people had settled themselves in one of the many bars and restaurant dotted around the city.

"What've we got here, then?"

Alfie dropped down beside the dog, and reached out a hand to stroke it, but the dog let out a deep warning growl and bared its teeth.

Something flickered in the teenager's eyes, something ugly and cruel.

Later, he thought. *Business first.*

"Right then," he said, cheerfully. "Have you had a chance to think about my offer? Because I don't think you heard me right, when we were chatting yesterday."

"I heard you fine."

Alfie giggled.

"It speaks! Look, lads, the spaz has a voice!"

The soldier looked at his animated face, imagined burying his fist in it, then remembered the kid was right. He didn't have the strength in his hands, anymore.

"I think the problem here is, you don't know what you've been missing. Does he?"

The men around him smiled, and began to move closer. Though the image was blurred, especially in his right eye, the soldier thought he saw a needle.

"This'll only hurt for a minute, mate. Then it'll be euphoric, I promise."

The dog stood up and snarled deeply, his body trembling, ruddy brown fur standing on end as he prepared to defend his new master.

"Get rid of the fucking dog," Alfie said.

One of the men brought out a retractable truncheon and raised it above his head, preparing to strike. The soldier and his dog both moved as one, the animal circling around, while the soldier raised himself to fight, one last time.

* * *

He was dressed entirely in black, in a Kevlar-enhanced bodysuit he'd commissioned from a contact in China. Looking at himself in the mirror, he thought he looked like Batman, or one of the other dark superheroes that society would never truly understand, but to whom they should be grateful.

Thanks to him, the streets were a better place.

He needed the ritual; he understood that a part of him—perhaps the only remaining part that was human—needed to think he was serving a purpose. It had to be more than bloodlust; more than the base desire to kill.

Some days, he really believed the lie.

He could spend many happy hours thinking of all his public service; but, as the recent police press conference had reminded him, society would never see it that way. The chief inspector would see him as a monster, some kind of freak.

And he would be right.

He heard a whimpering cry beneath his feet, and smiled to himself. There was no military exercise this evening—he'd already checked, and wouldn't make the same mistake again. There would be nobody to interrupt him, this time, and he wanted to make the most of it.

Whistling an old Northumbrian ditty to himself, he reached for the night vision goggles hanging on a peg beside the door and slid them around his neck, ready to put on when they moved outside.

He hoped she'd last a bit longer than the last one.

She'd been a terrible disappointment.

* * *

They came from nowhere.

Later, all the soldier would think was that his guardian angels seemed to materialise from nowhere; four men dressed in jeans and dark t-shirts, their faces concealed, and their arms covered in tattoos. They fell upon Alfie and his goons with all the force of a typhoon, using fists and knives and righteous anger to drive them away, grunting and hurling threats as they went.

He lay on the ground, curled into a ball around the dog, whose breathing was shallow after several kicks to the stomach.

Their leader came over to kneel beside him and spoke through the woollen ski mask.

"Y'alreet, mate? How bad are you?"

"The dog," was all he said. "The dog's hurt bad."

The man signalled the others, and they moved forward.

"Don't—don't hurt him," the soldier said, barely holding back tears. "Please."

"We ain't gonna hurt him, mate. We'll take him to the vet, how's that?"

The soldier looked away.

"I don't have the money to pay."

"It's on us, mate. C'mon, let's get going."

"How—how will I know he's alright?" the soldier asked.

"You're coming with us," the man said, and held out a hand to help him off the ground.

Through his hazy vision, the soldier's eye fell on a small tattoo on the underside of the man's wrist. It was small enough to be concealed beneath the cuffs of a shirt, but large enough for its meaning to be understood by those who knew.

It was a black circle, with three interlocking triangles.

"You coming then, pal? You deserve better than what you've been getting out here. I've seen you here before, and I know you were a soldier. We need good men like you—principled men. Will you join us?"

The soldier looked across at the dog, who lay cradled in another man's arms.

He took the hand that was offered.

CHAPTER 27

Almost giddy with the anticipation of what was to come, he moved the coffee table to the side and rolled back the woollen rug that covered most of the floor in the open-plan living space to reveal a trap door he'd personally cut into the floor. In the old days, when the stone tower had first been built, the basement beneath the wooden floor had been used as a cold store, for grain.

Now, he used it to store other things.

He paused, wondering what kind of mood he'd find her in. They were all purring and attentive, when they stuck their heads beside the window and asked if he was looking for business. They were smiling and polite when he gave them a smile and told them to hop in. Some of their smiles faded when he told them his place wasn't far, but he'd been blessed with the kind of features most women—and some men—seemed to trust.

Or perhaps, they *wanted* to trust.

It was remarkable, really, how many people overrode their natural, animal instinct at the sight of a half-pretty face, and the promise of a bit of cash in hand.

But then, they didn't value their own lives. They didn't know how fragile life could be, nor how easily it could be taken. They thought there would always be another day.

Not for Hayley.

She'd been a trusting one, all the way to the front door.

After that, she'd seen the shoes, and the fun had started.

Hot with anticipation, he reached down and took hold of a heavy iron handle, and pulled hard until the trap door opened and fell back against the floor with a loud thud of wood and metal. The opening was too high for them to reach it without a ladder, but he'd made one specifically for the space and he trotted back to the kitchen to get it.

When he returned, he fed the ladder through the entrance until he heard it hit the floor at the bottom, and then called down to the woman who awaited him.

"Hayley? Time to come out," he said, in the everyday tone of somebody discussing the weather. "Chop, chop—I haven't got all night."

When there was no response, he sighed.

They did this, sometimes. Passed out, or stayed silent, hoping he'd go away and leave them to die.

That's not how the game worked.

There was nothing that angered him more than the ones who found a way to off themselves, thereby depriving him of the privilege.

"Come on, Hayley—don't you want to know how to play the game? I'm a good sportsman, I promise—I'll play by the rules."

They were, of course, his rules.

When there was still no reply, he swore viciously and snapped his night vision goggles over his eyes. The basement had never been wired, which was how he preferred it, but it did make things slightly harder when he was forced to go down there and drag them out.

He peered down into the hole and took a sweeping glance around but could see no thermal light; only darkness. He patted the hunting knife tucked into the side pocket of his suit, and quickly descended the ladder. As his feet touched the floor, he spotted her, cowering in the corner that had been outside his line of vision.

"There you are."

It was an irritation to know she would be one of the weaker ones, whose fight had already gone before the game had even begun. Nonetheless, he must make do with what he had.

"Come on, princess. Time to go."

He walked through the darkness towards her and, at first, she saw his outline illuminated by the light that shone through the trap door. But, as he moved steadily closer, into the darkest corner where she waited, he seemed to melt into the blackness.

She closed her eyes, and listened to the sounds in the room.

Footsteps.

He'd taken seven, so far. Five or six more, and he'd be upon her.

Five, four, three…

She smelled his scent, felt his hot breath in the air around her face moments before his hand reached out to take her by the neck, hard and suffocating.

But she had been ready for this.

Her hand came up, bloodied and torn from the effort of working free the loose nails around the boarded window; the window that she hadn't been able to open in time. She gripped three of them between the fingers of her right hand and brought it up, aiming for his eyes.

They connected with something hard and solid.

Anger, fear, adrenaline burst through her body and she tried again, before he had time to react. Even as his free hand reached down for his knife, her left one came up to drag the goggles from his face, sending them clattering across the dark floor.

He let out a grunt of anger, and his hand tightened on her throat.

"That was *very* bad," he snarled, and she felt the spittle on her face as he lunged towards her in the darkness.

With tears leaking from her eyes, she brought her right hand up in one final effort, knowing that, if she failed, it would be her last.

* * *

She dragged the nails across his face, scoring through his skin so he reared back. It was not a serious injury, not enough to debilitate, but it bought her time—seconds, at most.

"*Bitch!*"

He lunged forward again, but she dodged him, her feet remembering the shape of the room. Her lungs were screaming as she dragged air into her body, her throat burning from where his hand had clamped the delicate skin. She moved like lightning, running towards the ladder, and heard his harsh breath at her heels.

But then, his footsteps slowed, and she heard him laugh again.

"Let the game begin," he said. "Go on, I'll give you a ten-second head start."

She didn't stop, but launched herself at the ladder, dragging her tired body up the rungs with only one thought in her mind.

Survival.

CHAPTER 28

They gave the soldier new clothes and a place to sleep, with fluffy pillows and a warm blanket. They'd made good their promise and had taken the dog to see one of their number, who worked at a clinic in the city and let them in through the back door. There, the dog had been x-rayed and checked, and the pain medication lifted from a locked box nobody would miss.

Now, the dog lay sleeping beside him in the cheap hotel room and he knew their kindness would come with a *quid pro quo* when they returned for him tomorrow, as they'd said they would. They needed an experienced soldier, someone who knew military strategy, they'd said.

What did they want with him?

He shook his head and reached for the remote to turn on the small television resting on top of a rickety chest of drawers opposite the bed. He enjoyed the novelty of flicking through the various channels, but the images were blurred to him.

He paused when he reached the late-night news and lay his head back against the pillow to listen.

"A briefing was held earlier today at the headquarters of the Northumbria Police Constabulary, where the Chief Constable offered her condolences to those affected by the recent spate of racially and religiously-motivated terror attacks around the city," the newsreader said.

The report cut to another woman's voice, presumably the Chief Constable, who spoke in an authoritative tone about how they would be tackling the violence.

But there would always be violence, he thought.

"Detective Chief Inspector Ryan joined the Chief Constable in expressing his sympathies to those affected and has advised people to remain vigilant to any suspicious behaviour, particularly parcels or packages left near places of worship..."

The soldier was almost drifting off to sleep, when the report cut to Ryan. When he mentioned an Odinist group, whose symbol had been left at the location of each of the three attacks, he sat up again and shuffled closer to the television screen. Still unable to see clearly, he stood up and peered closely at the screen, while the dog whimpered in its sleep and snuggled back into the warm spot he'd just vacated.

There, on the screen, was a picture of a symbol.

And he'd seen it before, on the underside of his new friend's wrist.

* * *

She dragged her body up the ladder and was almost blinded by the light in the room, her eyes having grown so accustomed to the darkness. Blinking, her heart hammering against the wall of her chest, she hurried into the room and looked frantically for a weapon. But then she heard the tread of his feet on the ladder below and she didn't stop to think but ran headlong towards the door and heaved it open, bursting out into the cold night air.

She ran blindly into the night, turning away from the road to run across the moorland, her feet bare against the hard, rocky earth below.

She felt nothing, but continued to run into the never-ending darkness, long legs eating up the ground as she thrust out into the unknown.

He snapped the night vision goggles back on his face and watched her from the pele tower, the whites of his teeth showing bright and hard as he smiled through the murky night air.

Run, little rabbit. Run.

* * *

151

She heard the warning shot, and felt the bullet skim past her face, missing the mark by mere inches.

She let out a sob and fell to the floor, her breathing ragged as she scrambled across the tufted soil, seeking shelter but finding none in the wide-open plains of the moorland.

Her torn fingers gripped the earth and she found herself crawling commando-style across the grass, driven by a strength she hadn't known she possessed.

She would not die here.

She would not die by his hand.

She heard another shot fire out into the night, not as close this time, and heard it connect five or six metres to her right. She wondered if he was toying with her, as he liked to, or whether he couldn't make out her exact position so low to the ground.

She crawled faster, not knowing where she was headed, and not caring, so long as she kept going. He was covering the ground fast, and she knew she didn't have long.

She was about to get up and run again, ready to take the risk, when her hand connected with something thick and very, very cold.

The heavy rain she'd heard yesterday had swelled one of the small burns that fed into the Coquet River, to the north of the Northumberland National Park, leaving the ground saturated with mud. The woman took a fistful of it in her hand and thought of the night goggles he wore, which picked up the heat.

He couldn't find her, if she wasn't emitting heat.

Frantically, she tumbled herself into the bog, immersing herself in the thick, cold sludge alongside the river. She crawled through it, heading east, following the line of the river which she knew would eventually lead to civilisation, if she survived that long.

She listened for the sound of his arrival but could hear nothing above the gentle babbling of the burn, one of a network that crisscrossed over the valley. Terrified, hardly able to breathe, she lowered herself as far as she could, tucking beneath the underside of the riverbank. The sound of mud squelching seemed deafening to her ears, and she began to shiver as the mud did its work.

She could see very little; only the silvery sheen of the starry night sky against the water, and her whole body froze in abject terror when she heard his voice, no more than a few feet away from where she hid in plain sight.

"WHERE ARE YOU?" he bellowed.

She closed her eyes and did something she hadn't done in a very, very long time.

She prayed.

CHAPTER 29

Sunday 18th August 2019

The following day brought with it more severe weather warnings, and Ryan awoke shortly before seven to find the rains had already begun.

"They're predicting severe storms over the next two days," Anna told him, while she brushed her teeth and watched him shave. "Be careful, if you're heading to Otterburn; you can get all kinds of flash floods and mudslides, in the Cheviots."

Ryan tapped his razor against the sink and started on the other side.

"Same goes for you," he said. "I have to go back into work today, but I'd feel better knowing you were with somebody. A woman was killed just a few miles from here, and the person who did it is still out there."

Ryan was a public figure, of sorts. After a run of high-profile cases over the past few years, his name and face were well known, especially in that part of the world. A certain class of criminal knew, only too well, that the finest way to punish him for doing his job was to hurt those he loved best.

Anna understood it, and had been on the receiving end, so she didn't bother to call him overprotective. If he was dishing out advice to the general public about staying safe, the least she could do would be to remain so, herself.

"I'll see what Denise and Samantha are up to, today. I can't imagine they'll want to hang around in Wooler, if the weather stays like this, and I'd love to see them both."

He wiped his face on a towel and turned to her with a grateful smile.

"Thank you," he said, and cupped her face in his hands to kiss her mouth. "I hope you know it has nothing to do with how strong I think you are, or how capable. It's just a question of safety in numbers, until I bring them in."

She nodded, but her eyes remained troubled.

"This one seems different, somehow," she said. "Are you worried in case you can't track him down?"

He could never lie to her, even if he wanted to.

"This one's like a cockroach," he said. "Resilient, in his approach. Prepared, and resourceful, capable of slipping into the shadows for long periods of time. I think he's mobile—either because he's with the army, and they move from camp to camp, or because he's a civilian, and has the kind of job that takes him away for some of the time. It's allowed him to operate discreetly, and to get to know his target areas very well. I have no doubt the man we're looking for is capable of stalking his prey for long periods of time, before making his first move."

She paled slightly, but he wasn't sorry. She needed to understand the gravity of the threat, so she'd be careful while he was gone. Anna was brave; she'd survived another madman's knife-blow, but that didn't mean she was invincible. She could bleed, just like the rest of them, and, if the unthinkable ever happened, it would kill him as well as her.

"What makes you so sure he's killed more than one person?" she asked, and he gave a slight shake of his head.

"I can't really be sure, until I have the evidence," he said. "But I feel it, *here.*"

He tapped his chest, roughly in the region of his heart.

"The shot was too clean," he said. "Too sure. He obliterated Layla Bruce's face, when he could have gone for the torso instead—which is a much easier shot to make, over long distances—because he knew it would take us longer to identify her. He's savvy, and obviously has an awareness of police and forensic procedures."

"You've beaten ones like him before," she said quietly. "You look at their mistakes, at their weaknesses, and you tug all the loose threads. You can do it again."

Ryan hadn't realised how much he needed to hear that, until she said it. To the world, he was a strong leader; an experienced man who always seemed to know the right thing to do, or to say.

But he still suffered self-doubt.

He was human, after all.

"Thank you," he said, and then spoke so quietly, she strained to hear. "With others, I've been able to find pity. On some very deep level, in a very small way, I've found it in my heart to pity the miserable creatures who've taken lives—even the most brutal ones. It's because they're victims, too, in their own way," he added, while she leaned against the basin and listened to him. "Either of their own mental health struggle, or of life. That isn't to say I excuse their actions; you know that I can't."

She nodded. Ryan had lost his sister to a notorious killer, five years ago, and the pain was still raw.

"I can't excuse them," he repeated. "But I can try to understand *why*, which helps a little, on those nights when I can't sleep."

There were many of those, she thought. The faces of the dead haunted him at night and she often heard him cry out; less so than he used to, but more often than she'd like.

"You think this one's different to the others?" she asked him. "Why?"

"It's hard to explain, but I'll put it like this," he said, running an agitated hand through black hair that was still wet from the shower. "With men like Keir Edwards, *The Hacker,* there'd been irreversible damage to his mind, when he was still a child. There are studies about things like that; about the effects of trauma on children before a certain age. It can prevent them from creating attachments with other people, or from feeling sadness or other normal emotions."

"Like brain damage," she said.

"Exactly. If that's the case, I feel an ounce of sadness for the child that they once were. I still hold the adult responsible, but a child isn't born bad. Killers aren't born; they're made, so they say."

"Is that what you believe?"

He nodded.

"It's what I've always believed, and it's what experience has taught me. But, when I think of this man, and of his motivations, I find myself wondering whether that's true for some, but not all."

"You're talking about evil," she realised.

Ryan looked at her for a long moment, then nodded slowly.

"Yes, I think so."

* * *

While Samantha continued to snore softly from her top bunk in the *Mystery Machine,* Phillips and MacKenzie seated themselves out of earshot, their voices muffled by the drumming of the rain against the roof of the campervan.

"I've just had a message from Anna," she said, scrolling through her phone. "She's asking if Samantha and I would like to head over and spend the day together."

Phillips smiled. The two women were great friends, but he could smell Ryan's hand in the sudden invitation, and that was no bad thing.

In fact, it saved him the job of having to think of an elaborate way to coax Denise into driving the campervan home—far, far away from the man who roamed the hills.

He cleared his throat.

"Well, seems like a nice idea," he said, a shade too casually. "There won't be much to do, if the weather carries on like this, and I don't think the vans will be out today to serve up Sam's daily dose of fish 'n' chips."

MacKenzie smiled, happy to humour him.

"There's always the swimming pool," she said.

He recovered quickly.

"Aye, but it'll be cold, getting out of there. No, you're far better heading over to keep Anna company. Maybe she's feeling a bit lonely and in need of company, what with Ryan being called away a lot this past couple of days."

MacKenzie's smile grew even wider.

"I suppose we could drive over," she said, and watched his shoulders relax again.

She leaned over to plant a kiss on the end of his nose.

"What was that for?"

"For caring," she answered simply. "Time was, I'd have missed being out on those moors with you—and I suppose part of me is missing the chase. But I'm on leave, and I intend to stick to it. I've paid my dues, and earned this time with Samantha."

"More than paid your dues," he murmured, and glanced down at the leg he'd been helping to massage. "How's it feeling, now?"

MacKenzie gave him a broad smile, so he wouldn't worry.

"Much better," she lied.

The truth was, the pain returned every day, and the exercises the physio had given her no longer made any kind of difference, and she was scared.

She loved to run, and to walk, and to swim.

She loved her work, which required a certain level of fitness despite her seniority. She missed the hard, lean strength she used to have, when she was kickboxing and doing pilates every day.

Now, she was lucky to manage once a week, and she was starting to think the effort was making her injury worse.

It was the anger that scared her the most. The weak, impotent anger of knowing she couldn't turn back time, so she'd never opened the door that day she was taken. She wished she'd known, somehow, or had some prescient, sixth sense to guide her.

But she hadn't, and she lived with the consequences now.

"Are you alright, love?"

She shook herself, and squeezed her husband's hand.

"I'll be just fine."

* * *

The soldier hadn't slept, for all the bed was cosy and warm.

He waged a battle in his own mind, between the boy he'd once been, and the man he was now. He remembered so clearly the day he'd enlisted; the excitement and promise of finding a *place* in the world, and of having a family for the first time. He remembered the laughter and tears of basic training, and the friends he thought he'd made for life.

He remembered sitting by the canal with Naseem, and of their long talks about the differences between their lives—and the similarities. Naseem, who had begun life as an orphan, on the streets of Lashkar Gar, and he, who'd begun life on the streets of Byker.

The memories ran through his mind like a showreel, both good and bad, as the hours ticked by and the dog continued to sleep by his side.

Before leaving him, the group had talked for over an hour the previous evening. They'd spoken of him having a place in the world again, and of having a *purpose* and the respect of his comrades. They talked about the erosion of 'good' values and the kind of society 'good' people should want to live in. Their leader had taken off his mask to reveal an average-looking joe, with thinning hair and pale blue eyes. He'd never made it into the Army, he'd said, and the others assured him it had been their loss; that he was a great military leader, nonetheless.

The leader, whose name was John, had asked him to join their cause. He told him they needed good men, with the right values. There would be a roof over his head, and food in his belly, for as long as he was with them.

And he'd been tempted.

Just the thought of never having to lie on the hard floor of the underpass had been enough; never having to beg for change or a kind word, ever again. They needed an intelligence man; somebody who could be invisible and go to all the places they couldn't. He'd be the one to do the recce, they'd be the ones to do the rest. He hadn't asked what 'the rest' would entail; he didn't need to.

Besides, he'd heard enough by then.

The leader said he'd be back to collect him in the morning, and they'd drive together to the place where the group met. It was more than a collective, he'd explained; it was a religion. They worshipped the god Odin, who would reward them in the afterlife, if they served him in the present. Their mission was simple and straightforward: they wanted an Aryan race, one which followed the only true faith. Theirs was an old religion, John said, and had existed long before the Christians came to despoil it. Such an old religion was deserving of an ancient monument; a proper and fitting place of worship to draw their strength.

And, he said, to celebrate the acquisition of a new bulk delivery of weapons.

After they'd left, the soldier thought of what it meant to defend his country, and remembered one very important thing.

His duty was to defend the United Kingdom from enemies *within*, as well as without.

He would not stand by, albeit broken and half-blind, to watch them burn all that was sacred and holy in the land where he'd been born. For all its imperfections, for all the disappointments and hurt, he'd been proud to wear his uniform, once. He remembered the feel and the weight of it, as well as the burden of it. He hadn't lost so much, and grieved so long, for a band of hate-mongers.

That isn't what he fought for—but it's what he would fight against.

CHAPTER 30

When Lowerson arrived at his desk at Police Headquarters, he opened his computer to find a stack of messages waiting for him. It was *always* the case that, following a televised police appeal, they received an influx of calls ranging from the bizarre to the ridiculous. However, it was *sometimes* the case that, hidden amongst all the fake confessions and false sightings, there was a hidden gem.

And, as he scrolled through the electronic notes taken by their call-handlers, his eye fell upon one in particular:

18.08.2019

06:42

Call duration: 1m50s

The caller wished to remain anonymous, but is described by the handler as male, approximately 30–50 years of age, with moderate North-Eastern regional accent / Geordie dialect. The caller sounded nervous, but delivered message clearly. Transcript follows.

OPERATIVE: You've reached the Northumbria Police non-emergency helpline. How can I help you today?

CALLER: I saw the report on the news about the Odinist group, and I need to speak to the detective in charge.

OPERATIVE: They aren't available at the moment, but will be back in the office during normal working hours. Can I take a message?

CALLER: Just tell them the group meets at the Duddo Stones at eight o'clock every Sunday night. There's at least four of them, and their leader's called

John. He's around forty, white, blue eyes, thinning hair, and slim build. He's the brains. They have that symbol, the one with the little triangles, tattooed on their wrists. They're fighters, with links to the military, and they say they're expecting a big delivery of weapons. They're planning more attacks this week.

OPERATIVE: Thank you for calling this in. Can I have your name, please, so the investigator can call you to obtain further information?

<CALL ENDS>

Lowerson pushed back from his chair and walked swiftly to the break room, where Yates was in the process of stirring milk into two mugs of tea.

"Mel? An anonymous call came through early this morning. The caller said the Odinist group meets at the Duddo Stones every Sunday night. They tried to warn us about numbers, and the fact they're fighters, some ex-military. It sounds genuine."

He referred to the Duddo Stone Circle, an ancient Early Bronze Age site of five large sandstones arranged in a circle just north of the tiny village of Duddo, less than five miles from the Scottish border.

"Today's a Sunday," she said. "So let's get authorisation to put together a sting."

"We don't have much to go on," he said.

"It's more than we had yesterday," she replied. "The Odinists in the south were meeting at Avebury Stone Circle and defacing the side of the stones, appropriating them for their own use. It makes sense that their northern contingent is doing the same thing, at a similar site up here."

"I never thought of Duddo," Lowerson said, and was mildly angry at himself. "It's out of the way, and not everybody knows about it. Mostly hikers, or people with a special interest in historic landmarks."

"It doesn't matter, we've got time."

"I wish I knew who called it in," he muttered, as they hurried along to the Chief Constable's office. "Whoever decided to pick up the phone has probably saved lives, not to mention thousands of pounds of property damage and untold emotional heartache."

"There are still some decent people in the world."

* * *

In another part of the city, Ryan and Phillips made their way along the stuffy, basement corridor towards the mortuary at the Royal Victoria Infirmary for the second day in a row. Even in their line of work, that was highly unusual, and neither man hoped it was the start of a new precedent.

"I'm surprised Pinter turned things around so quickly," Phillips remarked, as he fanned himself with the back of his notebook. The walls of the corridor were lined with enormous cylindrical fans that pumped out hot air, in an effort to keep the interior space of the mortuary very cold. The resulting effect was a corridor that felt very much like the Gobi Desert, in the summertime. "Normally, we have to drag him away from home on a weekend."

"He's being paid overtime," Ryan said, with a wry smile. "But aside from that, Joanne isn't back yet from Center Parcs. He has to find something to fill the long, lonely hours without her."

"Aye, and that's another thing," Phillips mumbled. "Do we even know if this woman's real? Has anybody ever seen her?"

Ryan merely shook his head.

"You're far too cynical. It wouldn't be the first time an attractive woman has fallen for the *dubious* charms of an older man, would it?" he said, with a pointed look in his friend's direction.

Phillips' mouth fell open.

"That's *completely* different," he blustered. "For one thing, I look at least ten years younger than my actual age, especially in soft lighting.

For another, Denise was practically chasing me around the office, I think you'll recall."

"Uh-huh," Ryan said. "I seem to recall you walking into pillars and doors whenever she was around the office, too."

On that note, he pushed open the double doors and stepped into the frosty interior of the mortuary, where Pinter was already waiting for them.

"You got my message, then?" he asked.

"You said it was urgent," Ryan replied. The pathologist had sent an email to him early that morning, requesting a consultation at his earliest convenience. Pinter could be theatrical, at times, but he was not prone to exaggeration.

"It's about the soldier—Jessica Stephenson," he said, and they saw that his eyes were bloodshot from a long night spent working on her post-mortem. "I've found something important."

He led them through the main mortuary space and back into the private corridor, where they'd viewed Layla Bruce, the previous day. This time, he opened Examination Room B, and ushered them inside. There was no bedside manner, this time, and he gave them no opportunity to prepare before he whipped back the paper shroud to reveal her purplish-grey head and shoulders.

Phillips let out a long, slow breath, and counted to ten inside his head, fighting a sudden wave of nausea. It was demeaning for a murder detective to have to admit to feeling squeamish at the sight of a corpse, but there it was.

Ryan took a long look at the woman's face, which now resembled a kind of glazed marble—it had a waxy white sheen about it, livor mortis having set in overnight whilst she was still hanging from a tree in the woods, causing the blood in her body to settle in her lower legs and feet. He was suddenly grateful to Pinter for not revealing that part of her body, which he knew would be horribly distended and almost black in colour.

Looking at the top half was hard enough.

The fine capillaries in Jessica's face had burst as she'd fought for breath during her final moments, leaving a web of dark lines just visible beneath her skin. Around her neck was a thick, angry line of purplish-black bruising, and her head rested at an odd angle on the examination table.

"Poor kid," Phillips muttered, and Ryan nodded.

He stood there for an endless moment, studying what was left of a bright, promising soldier who'd liked spy novels. His face was unmoving, and his jaw was hard, but his eyes were swirling pools of emotion when he turned back to the pathologist.

"What can you tell us?" he asked softly.

Pinter looked him dead in the eye.

"I can tell you, almost certainly, that she didn't commit suicide."

CHAPTER 31

Pinter's bombshell hung on the air of the mortuary examination room, suspended there with the chemicals swirling around their heads, before the two murder detectives recovered themselves.

"What do you mean, Jeff?"

The pathologist took a retractable pointer out of the pocket of his lab coat and clicked it a couple of times, before tracing it over a purple-black area of Jessica's neck.

"See here?"

Phillips took his stomach in his hands—quite literally—and shuffled forward a step or two, while Ryan peered down so he could get a better look.

"I'm sorry, I don't see anything unexpected," he said, eventually.

"It could be the advanced state of rigor mortis making things a little harder to see clearly," Pinter muttered, and walked back around to a computer which sat on a table by the wall. After a couple of fast taps on the keyboard, he brought up a series of close-up, enhanced photographs taken from the woman's neck as soon as she'd been admitted to the mortuary, the previous day.

"This may be easier for you to see," he said, and gestured both men forward. "Here's the part I was pointing out to you."

He was right, Ryan thought. The intervening hours had made a big difference, even though the mortuary technicians did their best to preserve the tissues.

"Yes, I can see more clearly."

"I still don't understand the significance," Phillips complained. "It looks like the shape of her belt buckle, when it tightened around the side of her neck."

"Exactly right," Pinter nodded, and clicked on another image of the belt, taken by the forensic team. "You see here, the belt has a silver, rectangular-shaped buckle?"

Ryan remembered holding it in his hands, having been the one to cut her down.

"Yes, it's standard issue for all privates," he said.

Pinter took them back to the first image.

"What you're seeing here is two injuries," he said, and turned around in his chair to explain. "When she first came to me, I couldn't understand why the buckle imprint didn't match the bruising and imprint of the one found around her neck. It's quite a distinctive pattern, you see; whatever was used to strangle her—I believe, a different belt—had an oval buckle, with a series of pins at the back, presumably where the metal was welded together, or where the manufacturer added some detailing."

He turned back to tap the screen, and they could see it now; five or six tiny purple dots, where the underside of the belt had dug into her skin.

"If you look at the belt that was found around her neck, you'll see it has no such detailing. It's a very simple design, with a larger buckle," Pinter continued. "You can see that it's made much less of a mark."

"Why?" Phillips asked. "Loss of circulation?"

Pinter nodded.

"Exactly, Frank. If the poor woman was already dead when that silver buckle went over her skin, there'd have been no blood circulating around her body. If there's no blood, she can't bruise."

Ryan felt a surge of anger so forceful, he needed to turn away and pace for a bit.

"You're telling me somebody strangled her using a different belt, and then tried to stage it as suicide, later, using Jessica's own belt?"

Pinter nodded again.

"It's the best explanation of her injuries," he said. "There are other evidential factors that add weight to my theory. Firstly, the fact there was no tree bark or leaf residue found on her skin or beneath her nails, whatsoever. I'd have expected to find at least one particle to show that she'd clambered onto the top of the quad bike and hoisted herself up onto that branch. It wouldn't have been easy."

Ryan considered the new information, and turned to Phillips.

"Frank, would you give Faulkner a call? I want to know his preliminary results from the scene in the forest yesterday. Particularly, around the quad bike."

"Use the landline in my office," Pinter offered. "There's no mobile signal, down here."

"Will do."

* * *

When Phillips returned a few minutes later, it was to confirm their worst suspicions.

"Turns out, Faulkner's been trying to call your mobile," he said. "Great minds, and all that. He's got an update for us, on both crime scenes."

Ryan waited.

"In terms of the quad bike, there are a few interesting details that he believes point towards a suspicious death. Firstly, there were no prints found on the quad bike whatsoever, apart from Jessica's right thumb and index finger, which were found on either side of the ignition key. However, that's highly unusual; firstly, because the prints were so complete and, secondly, because nobody inserts or turns an ignition key that way. They use the thumb and the *bridge* of the index finger, to support the key. It would be an awkward distance, otherwise."

Ryan pinched his two fingers together, and realised Faulkner was right.

"Somebody used her fingers to plant the prints on the ignition, and give the impression she'd driven up there herself?"

"That's what Faulkner reckons."

"You said there were a couple of things," Pinter prompted.

"Aye, there were. Those prints on the ignition key that are suspect, and the fact no other DNA or prints were found on the entire quad bike is unusual in itself. However, there are two really damning bits of evidence Faulkner's uncovered. The first is a small amount of blood, which was found near the back-left tyre, which he's confirmed belongs to the victim. The second is some partial footprints he found on the ground near the site. It's been fairly wet these past few days, so they managed to get a couple of decent casts that Faulkner thinks correspond to a size eight or nine walking boot."

"People tend to buy them a size up," Ryan put in.

"The point is, they don't match Jessica Stephenson's shoes, which were trainers rather than walking boots."

"That suggests she had no intention of going far," Ryan said. "As well as telling us there was another person present. Faulkner's sure it couldn't have been one of the soldiers who discovered the body—Amanda Huxley, for example?"

"Those witnesses claim they didn't touch or go near the quad bike area, which is where a lot of these partials were found," Phillips said. "But that's always subject to error."

Ryan nodded. Even factoring in the usual uncertainties, the evidence was certainly stacked in favour of murder, and that put an entirely different complexion on matters.

"We assumed Jessica Stephenson was troubled because she thought she was in some way responsible for Layla Bruce's death. Instead, I wonder if her anxiety was coming from another direction, or person. Frank, when we interviewed Huxley yesterday, didn't she say that Jessica had talked about needing to 'check' something?"

Phillips nodded.

"Everybody thought she meant the scene of the fatality, the previous day, but she might have been talking about something completely different."

Ryan looked down at the woman's body and grieved.

"We need to find out what she was checking, or what she knew, that was dangerous enough to get her killed," he said. "The probability is that it's one of her platoon."

"How d'you want to play it?" Phillips asked.

Ryan was staring at the picture of the belt marks on her skin, and tried to place where he'd seen somebody wearing such a belt before. An image skittered around the edges of his mind, just out of reach.

"We keep it quiet, for now," he decided. "I want whoever killed Jessica Stephenson to believe they've got away with it, so they'll relax and carry on as usual. In the meantime, we go back over all her personal possessions, Frank, and we chase up digital forensics, too. Have the team managed to unlock her phone, yet?"

Phillips nodded.

"We can collect it on the way back," he said. "We could draft in Jack and Mel, to help?"

But Ryan shook his head.

"They've got their hands full, with this Odinism investigation. They had a good tip-off this morning about a meeting taking place this evening, so they're working towards setting up a bust."

"He's come right, that lad," Phillips said, proudly.

"About bloody time," Ryan agreed. "But it means we're on our own with this one."

They thanked Pinter for his superlative efforts, and headed back out of the mortuary and into the rain.

CHAPTER 32

"You said Faulkner had an update on Layla, too?" Ryan asked, once they were back inside his car.

Phillips dabbed water from his face using the edge of his tie, which was a relatively sombre choice in comparison with his usual jaunty designs, being a dark navy blue with a pattern of tiny white stars.

"Oh, aye, that's right. He says the sniffer dogs were hampered by the rainfall, but they still managed to find blood spots from the underside of Layla's feet."

Ryan remembered they'd been bloody and torn.

"Anyhow, he's mapped the coordinates where the blood spatter was found, so we can have a look and see the general direction she was running."

"That's excellent," Ryan said. "Anything else?"

He had no sooner asked the question, when his phone began to ring. Ryan saw that it was the Control Room, and felt his stomach perform a slow flip.

"Ryan," he answered.

"Sir, we have a witness on the line by the name of 'Willow', who states she has information regarding your investigation into the death of Layla Bruce. Are you able to take the call?"

"Put her straight through," he said, urgently.

A moment later, he heard a beep, followed by the sound of a woman's voice. Even over the telephone line, he could tell she was frightened.

"Hello, this is DCI Ryan. Thank you for calling in, we appreciate it very much. Can you tell me your name, please?"

"Willow," the voice whispered. "I'm calling because I saw you on telly yesterday, and I saw the picture of Layla. Is it true she's really dead?"

"Yes, I'm sorry," Ryan replied. "Can you tell me how you knew Layla?"

"I—" He heard her swallow the nerves. "Um, we both worked in the same place."

"I'm sorry to put you on the spot, Willow, but it's important that I know the truth. Can you tell me, was Layla a sex worker?"

He heard a small sigh of relief from the woman at the end of the line.

"Yeah. We both were. I still am," she admitted.

"You told me you worked in the same place—where was that?" Ryan asked, and retrieved a small notepad from his jacket pocket.

"You promise you won't come for me?" she asked, in a voice that shook. "I need the money."

Ryan agreed.

"In that case, we used to work the patch around the back of the petrol station," she said, and named a spot just over the border, only a handful of miles away from where Layla's family still lived.

"How long had you both worked there?"

"Layla had been all over," she said. "In the early days, she had some pimp from Melrose who tried to take most of everythin' she made, and she thought she loved him. Told her some old tale about being a photographer, or something. Turned out he wanted her to do porno pictures, and all that. Eased her into the business, like they all do."

He heard her sigh down the phone.

"Anyway, we've worked the back of the station for the past six months," she said. "I don't know where she was before, she just said somewhere up north, near Aberdeen."

Ryan jotted it all down.

"This is very helpful, thank you, Willow. Can you tell me, when was the last time you saw her?"

"It was about six o'clock, maybe seven, last Wednesday night," she said. "There wasn't much happening, so I decided to drive over to the next station and see if there was any business there. She said she'd wait a bit longer where she was, and then follow me if she didn't have any luck."

Her voice broke a bit, as she remembered.

"I left her alone, and somebody took her."

* * *

Ryan spoke to Layla's friend for a while longer, consoling her and taking any other pertinent details she was able to share. When he hung up, he looked across to where Phillips was scrolling through a document on his phone.

"I asked one of the analysts to put together a list of all the missing women—especially those in the sex trade—who've gone from the area surrounding the Northumberland National Park, as well as any bodies that've been discovered in the last ten years," he said.

"And? Has it thrown up anything?" Ryan asked.

"As a matter of fact, yes."

Phillips leaned across the passenger seat, and showed Ryan a map.

"Two other women over the past three years have gone missing from the area, one of which we know to have been in the sex trade—the other one is less certain, but she was without a permanent address. The first went missing from here back in May of 2016." He pointed to a spot on the map near Berwick-upon-Tweed.

"Where's that?"

"It's a petrol station," Phillips replied, and sent alarm bells ringing in Ryan's ears. "The other lass went missing from…here," he said, pointing at another part of the map, not far from the village of Rothbury. "That was last year."

"I remember that one," Ryan said. "We looked at it for a connection with one of the cases we were working on at the time."

"Well, she's still missing, unfortunately. She was last sighted—"

"Don't tell me," Ryan interjected. "At a petrol station?"

"Bingo."

Ryan studied the map, and thought it was interesting that the earlier missing persons cases were the furthest distance from the National Park, whilst more recent cases had been closer to it. That seemed consistent with the general theory about serial killers' preferred geographic areas, but it didn't help them much, now.

"They sent through that list you were after, too," Phillips said, pulling up a different file to show him. "This is all the petrol stations they've been able to come up with so far, with links to the sex trade."

Ryan scanned the list, recognising some of the names and places as ones Willow had told him about, during their recent conversation.

He closed his eyes to think.

"Alright," he said. "Our killer likes to hunt in big landscapes, with plenty of space to hide. Where else is it possible to do that, other than the Northumberland National Park? Bearing in mind, he has an added layer of protection since the Army training ranges cover a chunk of that area, which means people are less likely to wander over his turf."

"One of the other training ranges?" Phillips said, immediately. "Or otherwise, some of the more remote parts of the Scottish Highlands, for example."

Ryan nodded.

"It seems to me that our killer prefers the north—perhaps he's tied to it, for work. Let's focus our attention on spaces like that over the border into Scotland. Get in touch with our colleagues in Edinburgh, and ask for the data on Missing Persons, specifically those in the sex trade, with links to any of the petrol stations on this list."

"Consider it done," Phillips said.

CHAPTER 33

Throughout the night, the woman remained hidden beneath the mud. She stayed there until she could no longer feel her limbs; until she became so cold, she was forced to move, or risk hypothermia and die anyway. Concealed by the darkness and the noise of the river, she'd crawled slowly east. She couldn't be sure where *he* was; she had no way of seeing or hearing him. For all she knew, he had seen her sad, slow struggle through the bog and was following only a few paces behind, waiting to take the perfect shot.

But it didn't come, and so she'd continued, the movement of her arms and legs providing some little warmth to raise her core temperature—enough to keep her alive, but not enough to be seen through the thermal lens on the goggles he wore.

She didn't know how far she travelled; she'd only known that she must never stop.

Eventually, though, the mud ran dry.

Forced out into the open again, she'd smeared cold mud on her body and kept low to the ground, moving at a snail's pace over the surface of the wide, empty landscape. She stopped dead when she thought she heard footsteps not far behind and stayed still, with her ear pressed to the ground as the rain began to fall.

Eventually, she'd moved again, making for a small patch of trees she spotted in the distance—so near, and yet so far away. If she ran, she would be there in under a minute; but, if she ran, he would see her, and she'd be dead before she ever made it that far.

And so, she'd continued to edge across the moor, her knees and feet so cut and torn, and her body so cold and weary, she thought she'd never make it. She floated in and out of consciousness, her body pushed far beyond its limits, but when she was lucid again, she pushed herself a little further.

Once, she thought she'd heard a gunshot further west of where she lay, and then another that sounded much closer, but she could no longer trust her own senses. Hyperawareness made her sick and shaky, and the impenetrable darkness played tricks with her mind.

The first light of dawn was beginning to rise behind the trees when her fingers touched the first pinecone on the forest floor, and she'd known that his night vision goggles would be of no use to him now. She'd been desperate to cry out for help, but knew it would be madness to make a sound in the silent valley.

Instead, she'd risked a glance over her shoulder.

In the early light of day, she'd seen not a single other living person.

There was nothing except endless land and sky and, in the far distance, the dim outline of a pele tower to remind her of how far she had come.

Not far enough.

She'd dragged herself into the protective fold of the forest and moved from tree to tree, her fingers clutching the bark for support as she went in search of shelter.

And later, when he picked up her trail and tracked her to the same spot, he saw the imprint of her hand against the tree and smiled.

The day was only just beginning, and he had all the time in the world.

He settled down to wait.

* * *

It would have been easy to take the dog and leave, the soldier thought, but that would have attracted suspicion. They'd know he'd contacted the police, and would have come looking for him, or cancelled their plans to meet at the Duddo Stones. If the police were to apprehend them, the group needed to believe they were still beneath the radar.

"I speak for all of us here, when I say we're glad you decided to join us," John, the leader, told him. "I know you'll be a tremendous asset to our company."

He enjoyed using military-sounding words, the soldier noticed, even though he'd never been in the services.

He could wear a tutu all he wanted, but it wouldn't make him a ballerina.

"How's your dog today, mate?" the other one asked, handing him a sausage and egg sandwich, wrapped in paper.

The soldier looked down at the dog, who was cradled in his arms on the back seat of the car, and stroked a tender hand over its nose.

"Better, thank you," he said politely.

"Don't mention it," John said, magnanimously. "We look after our own, don't we lads?"

There were obligatory murmurs of agreement around the large SUV.

"Right, well, I thought I'd take you over to see your new digs, then we'll pick you up again later on and take a trip up-country. Sound alright?"

The soldier nodded.

"Aye, thanks."

He listened as they talked over their plans for the coming weeks, and pontificated grandiose theories to support plainly fascist beliefs. He made the right noises and nodded whenever one of them should happen to glance his way but, all the while, he thought of Naseem.

He looked down at the dog to find it looking up at him, and thought he saw it smile.

CHAPTER 34

Back at Police Headquarters, Ryan and Phillips stole into the building like thieves in the night, bypassing the Chief Constable's hawk-eyed personal assistant and making directly for their colleagues in the Digital Forensics Department—affectionately known as the 'techies'. There, they retrieved Private Jess Stephenson's mobile phone, which had been unlocked, and the report on its contents—which included a long list of messages, photographs, social media content and books she'd downloaded to read on the journey between camps across the country.

There was a lot of John le Carré, Ryan noticed, and a bit of Frederick Forsythe.

Next, they went in search of Tom Faulkner, whose employers had recently purchased the rights to use the top floor of the building to facilitate easy discussion and reduce transportation between their high-tech lab space and the police evidence store. They made their way upstairs and found Faulkner hunched over a microscope.

"Morning, Tom."

Faulkner looked up and smiled.

"Been a long couple of days," he said. "Hard to tell what time of day it is."

Outside, the rain continued to pound the pavement, forming deep puddles in the staff car park. The sky was a uniform shade of grey, obliterating the sun so that the landscape appeared drab and dreary.

At least we'd finished the outdoor work," Faulkner said, counting his blessings. "I'm sorry, if you've come for any more news, I don't have anything for you, yet—"

"No, thanks, Tom. Phillips already passed on your update. We're here to see the personal items we took from Jess Stephenson's bunk area."

Faulkner raised an eyebrow.

"Of course," he replied, and reached for a box of disposable gloves. "You know the drill, by now."

They did indeed.

* * *

Thirty miles away, in Elsdon, Anna, Samantha and Denise enjoyed a rare moment of all-female company and threw themselves into the spirit of things with gusto. *Love Actually* was playing on the widescreen television, all of them having been in total agreement that it was a film 'for all seasons', and there was a pile of fashion magazines on the coffee table. Having raided Anna's collection of nail polishes, Samantha was presently treating the two women to a pedicure—of sorts—while the log-burner roared in the corner.

"Sweet Mary, Mother of…would you look at this, now?" MacKenzie declared, and showed the other two the page she was reading in a fashion magazine, depicting a woman with impossibly long legs wearing pink platforms whilst balanced on the edge of a boat off the coast of Capri.

"That's an accident waiting to happen," Anna grinned. "D'you ever think our lives aren't glamorous enough, Mac? Maybe we should get ourselves some pink platforms."

Denise snorted.

"What, and give up weekends in the *Mystery Machine* for long holidays in the Neapolitan Riviera? Chance would be a fine thing!"

"Well, Frank was thinking of Greece for your anniversary, but—" Samantha clamped her lips together and winced, belatedly remembering that it was supposed to be a secret.

"What was that?" MacKenzie asked, leaning down and wincing herself at the red nail polish smeared halfway across her feet.

"Argh! I wasn't supposed to say! I'm sorry, Denise…"

But MacKenzie was grinning like a fool.

"Sorry? That's the best news I've had all month," she said, and turned back to her friend. "Didn't I always tell you, Frank would never forget our anniversary."

As far as Anna recalled, MacKenzie had expressed serious concerns that, as Phillips struggled to remember any of the usual Hallmark dates in the diary at the best of times, there was little chance he would have remembered to book anything nice for their first wedding anniversary.

But she didn't say as much.

"He's a lovely man," she said instead, and then looked down at the girl who was now applying pink polish to her toes. "You've got a lovely family, Denise."

MacKenzie smiled and gave Sam's head an affectionate rub.

"We're lucky," she agreed, and then bit her tongue. As a woman herself, she knew there was very little that was more annoying than being asked when or if one planned to have babies.

All the same, she was curious, but the subject didn't come up again until much later in the afternoon, when Samantha had taken herself off to make a sandwich.

"We'd like one, Denise," Anna said, picking up the thread of their earlier conversation. "A family, I mean."

MacKenzie nodded.

"Well, there's plenty of time—"

But something about the way Anna had said it gave her pause.

"Want to talk about it?"

Anna turned to check Samantha was out of earshot, then spoke quietly.

"I've had three miscarriages," she said. "Ryan knows about one of them, but I couldn't tell him about the other two. I was too upset, myself, and I didn't want him to worry."

"Oh, darling."

MacKenzie held her arms open to her friend, and Anna let herself be held, drinking in the warmth before breaking away again to brush away tears.

"I don't know why I'm talking about this," she said, and gave a funny, self-deprecating laugh. "I suppose, I'm sick of people wondering."

"I'm sorry—"

"No, no, I don't mean our close friends, like you and Frank," Anna said, and gave her friend's hand a quick squeeze. "I mean all the women at work, who keep asking me when I'll be taking maternity leave, or the lady at the post office who keeps asking when she'll get to cuddle the baby. It hurts, Denise. It hurts badly, because I feel like such a failure."

"You're *not*," MacKenzie said, firmly. "There's no blame in this sort of thing, Anna. It's nobody's fault."

Her friend nodded, but wasn't altogether convinced.

"I keep wondering, what if we never can?" she said. "Ryan's been wonderful about it, as you can imagine. He says he fell in love with me because of who I am, not because of my breeding capabilities."

MacKenzie's lips quirked, because she could imagine him saying the very thing.

"He says he'll be happy if it's just the two of us, always," she said. "But it's me, as much as anything. I never felt broody before; I never understood the feeling all these other women talked about, because I just never felt it. I've always *liked* children, but I never wanted any—until I met Ryan."

"That makes sense," MacKenzie said. "It's logical not to feel the urge to procreate until you actually meet someone you want to do it with."

Anna smiled, and then heaved a sad sigh.

"It's a funny old world, isn't it?" she said. "You can spend a lifetime not wanting something and then, the moment you do, you find you can't have it."

"Yeah, it's funny how things turn out sometimes," MacKenzie agreed, and worked hard to keep any trace of sadness from her voice. This was not a moment to be gloomy.

"I went to see a specialist," Anna continued. "They're doing some more tests, but they think only one of my ovaries works properly. It doesn't mean I can't have kids, but it means the chances of natural conception are significantly lower."

MacKenzie nodded.

"There's always IVF?"

Anna nodded, and sipped her tea.

"You know," MacKenzie said. "I guess this means you'll just need to have lots and lots of *outstanding* sex. I'll venture to say, Ryan will be very…ah, *up* for the challenge."

Anna nearly spat out her tea, and gave her friend a playful swat on the arm as she hurriedly checked to see that Samantha was still out of hearing. But then, her lips curved into a smile and her eyes regained some of their sparkle.

"Well, every cloud, so they say," she said, and gave her friend a wink.

"Atta girl," MacKenzie said.

When Samantha stepped back into the room, she found the two women engrossed in the movie, their faces entirely too placid to be trusted.

"What did I miss?"

"Hugh Grant dancing," MacKenzie replied, and left it at that.

CHAPTER 35

From their perch on one of the high benches in Faulkner's lab, Ryan sifted through the box of Jess Stephenson's belongings, while Phillips went through the messages and photographs contained on her mobile phone. She'd lived a cleaner life than most, they were pleasantly surprised to find, and there were no helpfully large bank transfers to indicate she'd been blackmailing anyone—nor were there any helpful messages detailing a time and place to meet the person who'd go on to kill her. The last message Jess Stephenson sent was to her boyfriend, back in Cardiff, expressing her love and telling him she'd see him soon. Hardly the last words of someone about to kill themselves, even if they didn't have all the other evidence that pointed to murder.

Presently, Phillips paused and turned the phone this way and that.

Ryan looked up from his inspection of her clothes.

"Got something?"

"I don't know," Phillips said. "It seems odd, to have pictures of guns and all that on her phone."

"Not really," Ryan reasoned. "She was a soldier."

"Look at this," Phillips said, and held out the phone for Ryan to see for himself.

Sure enough, there were five or six close-up photographs of what appeared to be the interior of the armoury room, showing stacks of rifles and other types of handgun.

Something skirted around the edge of his brain, and Ryan suddenly dived into the box beside him, pulling out the copy of *Tinker, Tailor, Soldier, Spy*. He flicked to the back, where he had seen columns of figures, with dates at the top, the most recent being the date Jess's platoon had arrived at Otterburn. Beneath it, there was a series of numbers: 135, 135, 134, 134, 134, 129.

Six numbers, for the six days the platoon had been encamped at Otterburn.

"Frank, I think I know what she found."

* * *

"These figures represent how many of each type of weapon was present and accounted for, on each of the days the platoon has been at Otterburn," Ryan said. "As you can see, the numbers are decreasing slightly; just by the odd one, here and there."

"What are these other dates?" Phillips queried, looking at the other columns of figures in the back of the book.

"I think they're dates, and figures taken from the previous camps," Ryan said. "Jess must have suspected someone within her own company, not one of the standing officers at any of the camps. Frank, I need you to liaise with Major Malloy. Ask her to use some of her clout to speak to the previous camps and obtain figures for each type of weapon in their armoury. Ask if they're short. It'll be faster, and easier, coming from her. While you're at it, have a word with Jack and Mel. Tell them we might have found the military connection with the Odinist group—but we need a name. When they make the arrests, we need to know where the drop was being made, and by whom."

Phillips nodded, and made the calls.

"I've got something else for you, Ryan, but it relates to Layla Bruce," Faulkner called over, and then made his way across the laboratory.

"What is it, Tom?"

It doesn't add much but it does build up a picture," Faulkner said. "I've been going over some of the fibres and samples found underneath Layla's nails. A lot of it is plant and mineral-based, as you'd imagine after her trek over the moorland, but there was something else that was interesting. Eight of her nails had retained small particles of *stachybotrys chartarum*, otherwise known as black mould."

"I've sent a team over to the bedsit where Layla was living with a girl called Willow," Ryan said. "Maybe that's where it came from."

But Faulkner wasn't convinced.

"Even if she had it in her home, I don't know why she'd have it scratched beneath eight out of ten fingernails, unless she was clawing at it. I thought, more likely, she'd been held somewhere in a place of captivity, and that place had black mould."

Ryan nodded his agreement, eyes burning bright, and hoped they'd find whoever was responsible, before he took another.

* * *

Hayley used the cover of the trees during the day and walked as quickly as she could.

She stopped once, to sip some water from a puddle on the ground when she thought she might collapse, but did not allow herself to sit. If she did, she may never move again. There were 250 square kilometres of ground in the Northumberland National Park, much of it uninhabited—particularly on the army ranges. She could walk for days and never see another soul, which was, she supposed, why he had chosen this particular spot in the first place.

She continued to walk east and hoped she would reach a house, or a bothy, once she left the trees.

Anything at all.

Rain fell steadily, trickling through the forest until she came to the edge of an incline, at the bottom of which was another small river. She heard it bubbling away as the rainfall swelled its depths, and she watched it for a moment as she caught her breath.

At the precise moment she leaned down to rub her cramped legs, the gunshot ricocheted off the branch nearest to where her head had been.

She didn't stop, didn't give him time to pull the trigger again, but allowed herself to fall, rolling down the hillside towards the shallow river at the bottom.

* * *

He watched her tumble down the hill and ran across to the spot where she'd fallen, already reaching for another cartridge to reload his weapon.

His cartridge belt was empty.

He howled like an animal, his face contorting into something almost inhuman as he battled the terrible urge to use his hands, instead.

But that wasn't allowed.

If he broke his own rules, there'd be no telling what else he could be persuaded to do.

No, he thought. One bullet, straight to the head was more than sufficient. Anything more would be an indulgence, and he couldn't allow himself to become greedy. He'd seen what happened to those who lost control—they made mistakes, because they forgot basic principles. The game wasn't about accolades, or the pursuit of glory; it was a mission.

Even as he told himself the mantra, his fingers flexed by his sides as he watched the woman's body float on the river.

He looked up at the sky, then checked the time on his watch.

The sun was falling fast, now, and she couldn't go far. He'd be surprised if she hadn't broken at least one bone during her fall, and the river wasn't deep enough to cushion the blow. He only hoped she'd survived, so the fun could continue when he returned, fully reloaded and restocked.

He much preferred to hunt at night.

CHAPTER 36

W hen Ryan and Phillips received confirmation from Major Malloy that the last two camps where the 1ˢᵗ Royal Welsh Fusiliers had been stationed had both suffered losses to their armoury, they marshalled a small team of police officers and CSIs and drove directly to Otterburn Camp to instigate a search for a .308 Winchester rifle, as well as a belt bearing the distinctive markings found imprinted on Private Jess Stephenson's throat.

When the security guards at the outer gates saw that Ryan had brought a further two squad cars with him, a hasty radio message was conveyed to the CO, Lieutenant-Colonel Robson, who was waiting for them outside the main barracks when they arrived. Major Owen Jones was at his side.

Show of force, Ryan thought, and cast an eye over his own band of troops who surrounded him in equal fashion.

"Chief inspector? We didn't expect to see you out of hours," Robson said. "May I ask what's going on, and why you seem to have brought half of the constabulary with you?"

"New evidence has come to light regarding the murders of Layla Bruce, and of Private Jess Stephenson," he said, and watched the other man's face pale as the meaning of the words hit home. "We are authorised to search these premises and to seize evidence pertaining to our investigation. We'd be grateful for your cooperation in this matter, sir."

Major Malloy stepped forward.

"I'll start gathering officers in the Mess, so you can complete your search."

"Now, just hang on a minute!" Robson roared. "I'm responsible for what does and does not happen on this base—"

"Not when it concerns murder," Ryan said, simply, and gestured for his team to begin their work. "But, in deference to your rank, I'll conduct the search of your room myself."

Without another word, Ryan stepped around the CO and jogged up the short flight of stairs leading into the Officers' Quarters.

* * *

As the North's equivalent of Stonehenge, the Duddo Stone Circle was an impressive feat of engineering, each hunk of sandstone having been erected over four thousand years ago atop a site which enjoyed unparalleled views of the Cheviot Hills. It rather put to shame some of their more recent architectural achievements, Lowerson thought, as he and Yates made their way along the winding road to the small village of the same name, shortly before eight o'clock.

"The other units are in position," Yates said, following a brief radio exchange. "Apparently, there's seven of them up there already, and it's raining cats and dogs."

The Stones were a kilometre's walk from the roadside slightly north of Duddo, and the plan was for police vehicles to remain concealed until they could be reasonably sure that all those members of the Odinist group who planned to attend had already arrived. It reduced the chances of them being spotted too soon, and gave the police an opportunity to disable the group's vehicles while they were up beside the Stones, dancing in the rain—or whatever it was they planned to do.

"Well, I suppose we can say they're dedicated," Lowerson remarked, looking out at the monsoon weather conditions. "I wouldn't want to be caught out in that for long."

* * *

The woman touched Death's hand, and let it go, one more time.

The femur in her left leg fractured as she fell into the icy-cold waters of the river below, connecting with the hard riverbed that had been formed during the last Ice Age.

She hadn't thought about whether to jump; she'd simply done it— the thought of choosing her own death far preferable to giving *him* the twisted satisfaction he craved.

But now, she knew her body could not go on as it was; her fingers were blue and, without any sunlight to warm them, her muscles were seizing and contracting, making it impossible for her to walk, even discounting the shooting pain in her leg.

Darkness was setting in quickly now, and she knew she would not last another hour, let alone another night, if she could not get warm.

Convulsing with cold and pain, she saw salvation in the field up ahead, and knew she had to find the strength to do what she must do.

Survive.

* * *

Ryan and Phillips searched the CO's private quarters with single-minded intensity, while the rest of their team went about the business of searching the remaining officers' quarters. However, when more than an hour passed by and they had not found either the rifle or the belt they sought, Ryan began to think they had been disposed of elsewhere.

"Who's responsible for keeping a log of the weapons in the armoury?" Ryan asked the Lieutenant-Colonel.

"Ah, well, we have a rota of officers who take responsibility for that," he replied. "Why do you ask?"

Ryan did not answer directly.

"Have you been made aware of any discrepancies in the logbook?"

The CO frowned and shook his head.

"No, none whatsoever," he replied. "Well, I mean, I know that one or two had to be decommissioned because they were misfiring, and some have been sent back to the manufacturer for repairs, but that's all I'm aware of, chief inspector."

He paused, frowning as they dug through his underwear drawer, and turning an unhealthy shade of red when they came across his stash of 'special' reading material.

Ryan cleared his throat.

"Must be difficult, being away from home for long periods at a time," he said, and thought of Layla and Willow, and all the other girls like them.

"Quite," the CO said, testily.

"Nothing here," Phillips said, and straightened up again while Ryan agreed there was nothing behind the dresser, either.

Just one place left to look.

"May we see the belt you're wearing, sir?"

The CO looked thoroughly confused but complied with the request and lifted the khaki jumper he wore to reveal a standard, brown leather belt with a rectangular buckle.

CHAPTER 37

The soldier stood in the shadow of one of the Duddo Stones, huddled inside a raincoat. He'd left the dog on the back seat of the car with a small bowl of food and water, and the window cracked to allow for air circulation. He wished he could check on him, but instead he was standing in the pouring rain, listening to the rantings and ravings of a group of deeply disturbed individuals.

He missed the underpass.

Aside from the group's leader, John, all of the other men were skinheads. They were all-male, all-white and all, unbelievably, dressed in knock-off boar skin cloaks he strongly suspected to have been made from bits of old carpet. They'd given themselves new names, too, and John had told him that, when they were in this special place, he was no longer 'John Dobson'; he was '*Ragnar* Dobson'.

The soldier had relied on his scars to help him keep a straight face.

The rain continued to fall as *Ragnar* bleated on about far-right racism and neo-fascism being the bedrock of their 'race vessel', mythologizing the virtues of European white males, so they were no longer average white men with beer bellies and receding hairlines, but heroes in their own minds, speaking of the genetic ties between them and of their bold, fearlessness.

The soldier could barely stomach it when the discussion turned to historic references to the Third Reich, nor when John—*Ragnar*—spoke of adopting the same initiation rites as had been used by Hitler's Schutzstaffel.

He looked around to see if there was any sign of the police, but he could see little beyond the blanket of cold rain, and the mist which rolled in from the hills and curled its way around the stones.

The proselytising continued, until he heard his name and the group turned as one to look at him.

"*We welcome our newest folk brother,*" John was saying. "*Nobody can know better than him, the indignity of suffering such loss, in the name of those whose faiths and customs are so far beneath our own…*"

The soldier felt the old anger rise again, and he welcomed it, rejoicing in the knowledge that he could still feel strongly about the things that were important, and worth saving.

"I was proud to fight for those people," he said, and his voice rang out clearly across the misty hillside. "I'd do the same again."

John, who believed himself to be the great Viking King Ragnar's direct descendant, looked at the soldier and wondered whether it was time to enact the blood rite he'd been hoping to introduce to the group, sometime soon.

Before he could suggest it, he caught sight of dark figures through the gaps in the stones, walking through the mist towards him. Some of them were armed with weapons from the Tactical Firearms Unit at Northumbria CID, and they shouted a warning.

He turned around the circle, looking for somewhere to run, his 'boar' cloak flapping around his face, and his followers looked on as their great leader tried to hide behind the stones, desperately seeking a way out rather than dying the noble, Viking Warrior's death that would ensure his place in the Great Hall of Valhalla.

The only hall he'd be spending any great amount of time in would be the dining hall, at Her Majesty's Pleasure.

* * *

"I'm told you were the one who made the phone call to CID."

The soldier looked up to see the blurry face of a young man in his early thirties, holding Naseem gently in his arms. He was seated in the back of one of the squad cars, because none of the arresting officers had believed his story about having been the one to call it in, that morning.

He nodded.

"I'm DC Lowerson, of Northumbria CID," the man said. "Thank you for making that report—it made all the difference to us."

Lowerson held up the dog.

"I think this is yours," he said, and deposited the sleeping animal carefully in the soldier's arms. "Does he need anything? Do you?"

He shook his head.

"I'll need you to come along to the station and make a statement, if you don't mind," Lowerson said. "We'll give you a ride."

The soldier followed him across to an unmarked car parked on the verge across the street.

"They said they were planning to pick up a delivery tonight," he said, and Lowerson nodded.

"We got it all," he said. "We had some mics set up by the sides of the stones. Did that bloke really call himself *Ragnar?*"

The soldier grinned.

"You couldn't make this stuff up," Lowerson muttered.

"I've remembered something else," the soldier said, suddenly.

Lowerson's smile faded at the urgent tone.

"What's that?"

"They said they didn't know *her* name. The one who'd be making the drop. They said *her.* I don't know if that helps."

* * *

Ryan and Phillips had just stepped into the Officers' Mess, when the call came through.

As Phillips proceeded to go through the usual motions of apologizing for any inconvenience, his voice stalled when Ryan raised a hand and indicated he should hold off.

A moment later, Ryan ended the call, and turned back to face the small assembly.

"Thank you for your patience, which is much appreciated. At this time, I'd like all the female officers to take a step forward, please—"

He broke off, when he noticed one of their number was missing.

"Where's Sergeant Major Davies?" he asked.

"I think Gwen just popped to the loo," Corporal Huxley said. "I'm sure she'll be back in a minute."

But a minute turned into two, and she did not come back.

Ryan sent a female officer to look for her, who returned in under a minute, slightly out of breath.

"She's not in the ladies' room, sir. She's not in her room, either."

Ryan looked out of the window facing the central courtyard, and watched as Davies reversed one of the Jeeps out of its parking space and then hit the accelerator with a squeal of tyres.

He turned to the CO and pointed his finger.

"Get onto the security guards at the front! She's not to exit those gates!"

Robson spoke swiftly into his radio, and received a response.

"They have orders to open fire to immobilise the vehicle," he said, and Ryan didn't stop to worry about that, but turned on his heel and flew from the room, with Phillips in tow. He almost barrelled into Major Malloy, who was walking up the steps to join them.

"It's Davies!" Ryan shouted. "She's taken a Jeep and she's going for the front gates, but they're blocking that route. I need you to make sure the other access roads are barred at every checkpoint!"

Malloy didn't question it, but flew into action, running across the courtyard to issue orders.

Seconds later, they saw Davies' Jeep perform another dangerous reversing manoeuvre, before accelerating back down the hill towards the base. Those who had run outside threw themselves back as she drove straight through the courtyard, her face focused only on escape, her eyes wild with panic.

"I don't understand this," Huxley said. "Gwen wouldn't hurt anyone—"

"She's a bent soldier," Ryan snapped, as he scanned the area for a suitable vehicle. "Treat her as any other dangerous target."

Malloy had deployed a number of army personnel in Jeeps to all the major checkpoints around the ranges, and he'd admired her skill and speed in making that happen. But consequently, there were no off-road vehicles left, and he knew that, if Davies found the army access roads closed, she'd be forced to go cross-country, instead."

"Quad bikes?" he asked, of the officers who had gathered in collective shock by the foot of the stairs.

"Here!" Dalgliesh threw a set of keys to Ryan, which he caught one-handed. "It's number 8, over there."

Phillips took a set of keys from Corporal Huxley, and then they were jogging across to a line of heavy-duty quad bikes.

"We'll try to keep her in sight!" Ryan called back. "Get a detachment to follow us as soon as you can!"

The CO nodded.

"Be careful, son."

Ryan paused for a brief second, then nodded.

"Thank you, sir."

CHAPTER 38

For the first time in a long while, Phillips kept pace with his younger friend as they ran full pelt across the tarmacked courtyard towards the quad bikes that were parked in a kind of carport on the far side. Their boots skidded against the wet floor as the storm raged in the darkening skies above, and both men felt a frisson of fear as they mounted the bikes and prepared to drive out into the unknown.

They had phones, night goggles and compasses—as well as maps and radios tucked into the inner pockets of their weatherproof jackets—but before they left, Dalgliesh rushed back out with two service pistols, similar to the ones Ryan and Phillips were familiar with from their specialist firearms training.

"Protect yourselves," he said. "Gwen will be armed, and she's one of our best marksmen. Don't take any risks."

Neither man relished the prospect of using a weapon, and neither had been called upon to do so before, but out on the moorland it was each man—or woman—for himself.

Both men shoved one in the pocket of their coats.

"Remember to follow the rivers, if you lose your way. She's already tried and failed to get through the first couple of checkpoints along the western perimeter. We've got tactical teams in place all the way along both sides, so there's nowhere for her to go, except deeper into the ranges."

Ryan nodded, and then gunned his engine.

"Then that's where we'll go. Ready?" he asked of his sergeant.

Phillips nodded.

"I'll be right behind you."

They raced out into the storm.

* * *

As they polished off the last of a box of particularly fine Belgian truffles and watched the final scenes of *Notting Hall*, Samantha turned to Anna and Denise.

"When Ryan and Phillips came along to do that talk for my assembly at school, they made their jobs sound really boring," she said. "They said it was mostly looking over files, or speaking to witnesses and all that. I thought it would be a bit more exciting."

MacKenzie thought of all the scrapes she'd managed to get into during her time at Northumbria CID, and pasted a smile on her face.

"It's mostly about science and forensics, these days. We hardly ever get to go on exciting car chases, or anything like that."

"That's a shame," Samantha said. "Do you think that's why they're so late—because they're looking over statements and stuff?"

"Probably," Anna said. "Ryan will be bored to tears."

* * *

Ryan took the small tufted ramp at speed, and felt the quad bike fly through the air, before crashing back down again with a growl of its engine. He was in a half-standing position to afford a better line of sight over the top of the handlebars, relying on his old motorcycle training through the streets of Florence to stay in control.

Phillips followed behind, his body taught and focused, keeping pace with his friend while a large searchlight fixed to the front of Ryan's quad guided the way. It was exhausting work, not only to keep the vehicles on course but to keep concentrating on the passing landscape as the rain beat down upon their backs and ran into their eyes.

Then, Ryan slowed his quad a fraction and pointed north-west, to where he'd seen a large thermal mass travelling north.

Gwen Davies.

Phillips raised his hand in a 'thumbs-up' signal and turned his bike as Ryan did, steering it around the deeper gullies and larger boulders until they were back on open plains again and could ramp up the speed.

* * *

The woman had stopped shivering sometime in the past hour, but now the tremors had started up again. It was probably shock as much as cold, and the warmth that the dead sheep had lent her was starting to wear off.

She'd have to find another one.

She didn't know herself anymore—this broken person, this sheep-killer. She didn't recognise the woman she'd been, only a couple of days before, and she didn't know how she'd ever return.

She only knew how to survive.

The field was full of hefted sheep, their tubby, well-fed bodies ragged with wool she wished she had the strength to rip from them.

She'd found a dip in the land, just wide enough for her to lie in, and had dragged the sheep over to it, tugging its still-warm, woollen body over the top so it became something of a tomb. She hadn't known if it would work, but she knew she had to try, and had taken the sheep's skull in her weak, shaking arms and twisted it with a sharp *crack*.

She would never be the same again, even if she survived.

She would never forget the sound.

* * *

Their quads bumped and skidded over the ground, but they were faster than Davies' Jeep, which couldn't swerve to avoid the smaller hazards. Ryan knew they were gaining on her and pressed onward, never taking his eyes from the valley floor, ready to take evasive manoeuvres if need be.

He glanced back at Frank, who signalled onward, and found himself grinning fiercely.

No matter how many bacon stotties that man ate, he would always remember the sight of him flying across the Northumberland National Park on a racing-red quad bike with the storm blowing a gale through his hair. There were few people Ryan could really trust, but Phillips was one of them, and there was nobody he'd rather go into battle with.

The Jeep made a sudden stop up ahead, and Ryan raised a hand to signal caution as he slowed his quad right down to a crawl.

As they drew nearer, they could see the driver's door was wide open, and the Jeep was empty.

A second later, they heard the whizzing sound of a bullet popping through the air, and the bright spotlight on the front of Ryan's quad burst into shards of glass, nicking the skin on his hands and removing their main light source.

Ryan rolled off the quad and saw Phillips doing the same, using the side of the vehicle for cover.

"GWEN!" he called out, and his voice echoed around the valley like a yodel. "IT'S OVER, GWEN! PUT YOUR WEAPON DOWN, AND GIVE YOURSELF UP!"

Ryan waited, but there was no response.

He repeated his instruction and, at Phillips 'OK' signal, reached for his weapon, cocked it above his head and fired a single warning shot.

CHAPTER 39

Ryan heard nothing after he'd fired the warning shot, so he risked glancing around the side of the quad bike. When he saw nothing, either, he signalled to Phillips that they should proceed with caution.

They emerged from their makeshift cover and found the Jeep empty, with the keys still in the ignition. Ryan leaned inside and turned off the engine, but left the headlines on, while Phillips stayed low and then moved quickly across to join him, where both men flattened themselves against the side, keeping their weapons raised.

"Where's she gone?" Phillips wondered.

There was a thundering sound of water nearby, louder than the fall of the rain against the valley floor. They followed the sound, wondering if Davies had hoped to cross the river and escape capture on foot. When he'd moved a safe distance from the headlights, Ryan slipped his night goggles back on and used them to scan the area, seeking out any heat sources, but finding none.

When they moved closer to the crashing sound of water hitting rock, they understood why Gwen Davies had been forced to stop her car.

The river had burst its banks and was rising fast, gushing from the hills and down into the valley below.

"There!" Ryan cried, shoving wet hair from his eyes as he pointed towards the flailing figure that was clinging to the edge of the crumbling riverbank.

Regardless of what Sergeant Major Gwen Davies had done, it did not occur to either man not to help her. There would be no honour in that, and there would be no justice for Private Stephenson's family, either.

Whether they *could* help her was another matter.

She was clinging to some grassy reeds on an outcrop of land that hadn't yet broken away, but appeared very precarious. Leaving Phillips for a moment, Ryan sprinted back to the Jeep and opened the boot, searching for a length of rope.

Once he found it, he hurried back and started to knot one end around his waist.

"No, lad! It's too dangerous for you to go in!"

Ryan was no fool, but he was accustomed to taking calculated risks. His eyes scanned the rapids with calculated precision, and he pointed to what he judged to be the safest point.

"You stand on firm ground on this side," he said, raising his voice to be heard above the rushing water. "Take the other end. I'll lean over and see if I can reach her, then we'll both pull her in."

Phillips nodded, and they set off to where Davies clung to the grassy edge, trying to heave her body to the side and away from the main thrust of the water. Feeling his way through the darkness, Ryan lowered himself onto his belly and shuffled as far out as he dared, feeling the water splash into his face again and again.

He held out a hand to Davies, once he was sure Phillips had a solid foothold.

"TAKE MY HAND!" he shouted.

But still, she clung to the reeds, apparently unable to move, or in some kind of shock.

Ryan tried again, edging a little further out, so more than half of his body was resting on the precarious piece of earth that the river had not yet taken.

Davies looked up at him, and he saw terror writ large on her face.

There would be time enough for recriminations later, but he held out his hand again.

This time, she took it.

* * *

He heard shots being fired on the south side of the river and stopped dead, crouching low in case anyone should see. It had taken longer than expected to return to the pele tower, but it was almost in sight now. He had a good idea of her location, so he would take the van to shave off some time on the way back out.

However, he hadn't counted on another live-fire exercise.

There had been no mention of any army training exercises on the website listing, but he was *certain* he heard shots being fired.

It was a challenge, but it would make the hunt all the more interesting.

* * *

From her woollen cocoon, the woman heard the faint sound of a gunshot, and her whole body froze while she played dead—as dead as the sheep.

Had he come for her, again?

He hadn't fired a warning shot the last time; he preferred not to waste his bullets and took shots that were meant to hit their mark.

A pity for him that he missed.

Her body was a solid wall of pain; every part of her was in agony, but she realised that was a good thing, because her body had thawed sufficiently to be able to *feel* again.

She heard a second shot, and a thought occurred to her.

Perhaps it wasn't him, at all.

She'd become so accustomed to the pain of rigidity inside her makeshift coffin, the woman had begun to contemplate letting herself die, there beneath the weight of the wool. At first, she'd planned to use it for warmth, and for camouflage, if he was to come looking for her again. Then, she'd wondered how she would ever make it across the plains with an injured leg, except with extreme difficulty. She had no way of knowing where she was, or where she was going, so she'd probably die there, no matter which way she turned.

Then, that quiet voice rose up again inside her; the voice that spoke only one word:

Survive.

CHAPTER 40

The land broke away just as Ryan was heaving Davies from the water.

They both fell suddenly, headlong into the freezing water that wanted to sweep them both away.

Ryan clung to her arm, keeping an iron grip, while Phillips heaved against the power of the water with all the strength that he had.

But it was not enough, and the force drove him to the floor, the unexpected action dragging him along the riverbank and crashing into the water himself, where he was immediately caught in the fast-flowing current.

Fear like a vice around his heart, Ryan thrust out towards the other side of the river, feeling the rope tighten around his waist and knowing that, somewhere at the end of it, Frank was still attached. Ryan grabbed tightly onto one of the exposed roots beside the northern bank and held on for grim life, the muscles in his arm screaming while his other arm still held fast onto Davies. Swallowing mouthfuls of water, he looked at her and then at the root he was holding.

She nodded her understanding.

Striking out against the current, she swam against it while Ryan kept a hold of one arm, supporting her against the current using his own strength, until she could take hold of the root as well. When he was sure she had a tight enough grip, he let go of her arm and then nodded again.

She leaned on the root and used it to boost her body up the side of the bank, choking on water as it rushed into her mouth and nostrils, her tired, cold feet slipping against the mud as it ran down the sides of the bank and into the water. When her body was trembling and unable to go any higher, Ryan cried out and thrust upward, pushing his free hand into the small of her back to give her the final boost she needed to clamber out.

Ryan clung to the root with both hands, fighting the pull of the rope to hold his position while he blinked water from his eyes and tried to spot Frank at the other end.

Desolation swamped him, when he couldn't immediately see his friend—the best friend he'd ever had—and grief was raw.

He sobbed, tears running as fast as the river water, and then he felt a tug on the line that was nothing to do with the river.

Frank was alive.

* * *

By the time Ryan and Phillips managed to haul themselves from the water, shaking and exhausted, they found Davies collapsed and unconscious by the riverbank, apparently having tried to flee once again.

"Ungrateful madam," Phillips wheezed, and then proceeded to cough a lungful of water from his body.

Ryan did the same, every muscle in his body trembling.

When they had recovered themselves sufficiently to check that Davies was still alive, they realised almost everything of use had been washed away by the current, or damaged, including their phones and radios.

Ryan looked around to try to get his bearings, and remembered what Dalgliesh had told him about the positioning of the rivers. The small, laminated map was inside his weatherproof jacket, and he brought it out now, holding it up to the sky this way and that, to try to read it.

But it was no use.

Left only with his sense of direction, Ryan knew what he needed to do.

"We need to get somewhere with more shelter," he said. "I'll start a fire for you there, and I'll go off to find help. It can't be far, and reinforcements shouldn't be far behind, either."

Phillips wanted to protest, but he knew they couldn't go together; somebody needed to stay with Davies.

He nodded, and together they lifted her, panting up the hill towards higher ground, where they could see the outline of a house in the distance.

Ryan sent up a prayer to a god he didn't believe in, and put a hand on Phillips' shoulder.

"Stay here and try to keep moving," he said. "I'll be back soon."

* * *

Ryan forced his legs to move, and he managed to work up to a jog, running as fast as he could to warm his muscles and get back to his friend as quickly as he could. Up ahead, the outline of an old-fashioned pele tower came into view. They were common in the border regions, the small, fortified tower houses having been built mostly during the fourteenth and early seventeenth centuries to resist attack from reiving families on both sides of the border. Nowadays, people liked to rent them as holiday cottages, or renovate them as family homes, but he hadn't expected to find one inside the Controlled Area.

As he drew closer, he saw that this one was quite small, but there was a light burning in the window, which told him somebody must be home.

Reaching the top of the hill, he saw there was a van in the driveway with a large logo depicting an image of a laughing, cartoon cow wearing sunglasses.

Smiling at that, Ryan hurried over to bang loudly on the front door.

When there was no answer, he tried again, and then moved to peer inside one of the narrow windows, but they'd been designed to repeal attackers, and they were too high for him to reach.

Ryan walked around to the back of the house and found that its owner had left the back door open. He couldn't picture any nearby villages where one might conceivably pop out to buy a pint of milk, but perhaps they had rural neighbours and had gone to visit them instead.

He turned the handle and stepped inside.

CHAPTER 41

As soon as Ryan stepped over the threshold, he sensed something was wrong.

There was a scent to the air that he recognised; the unique scent of death that every murder detective came to know and was thereafter never able to forget.

He looked around for a weapon and saw a block of knives, so he pulled out the largest and held it, commando-style, beside his thigh. Ryan moved carefully through the rooms, never forgetting his training, until he reached what was obviously the main living area.

He saw the shoes, first.

At least twenty pairs of women's shoes had been proudly arranged on the wall, to resemble the stuffed animal heads you sometimes found in old manor houses. He didn't think there would be too much trouble identifying their original owners, since each bore a small plaque with their name and the date the shoes had been taken, as well as a tiny set of engraved coordinates.

Their place of execution.

Ryan felt bile rise in his stomach, and he started to back away and out of the room when he spotted that a large antique rug had been pulled back to reveal a trapdoor, which lay open. Stepping closer, he saw a pitch-dark place with foul air, and knew that this was where Layla Bruce had come into contact with black mould.

Raising his head, Ryan looked at all the shoes on the wall until he found the most recent pair, which had no plaque, yet.

He turned to find a telephone and put an emergency call through, his eyes scanning the surfaces and corners, when he heard a key turning in the front door lock.

There was no time to run before it swung open.

* * *

The two men faced each other across the room, assessing the threat in the nanosecond it took for Ryan to understand that the man held a hunting rifle, whilst he was unarmed except for the carving knife—the army pistol having been washed away in the river.

No words were said.

As the killer raised his rifle, Ryan lifted the knife and hurled it across the room. The man dodged it easily and pulled the trigger.

The air left Ryan's body in a long rush as he realised the man was out of ammunition, and he was still alive.

There was no time to celebrate—he saw the man reach for a fresh handful of cartridges from an open box nearby, and Ryan moved like lightning. He threw himself behind the sofa in time for the first shot to fire, and heard the explosion of cushions around his head. He kept moving, hurling odds and ends in the man's direction as he raced for the back door, hearing another bullet go past his ear before he burst back outside and beneath the cloak of darkness.

Ryan raced away from the house, legs pumping to cover the ground quickly and warn Phillips. Then, he remembered Frank's situation—he was a sitting duck, on the floor with an injured woman. Breathing hard, his lungs dragging air into his body, Ryan changed direction and moved in a wide semi-circle to the east.

He thought the darkness would act as a shield, but he'd forgotten Layla Bruce.

This killer liked darkness.

* * *

Ryan knew that there would be no chance of outrunning a bullet, especially on the wide, open plains, so there was only one other place he could go that would protect him from the night vision goggles, and put a greater distance between him and his pursuer.

Back in the river.

He zig-zagged as far as he dared, feet sliding against the sodden earth, and was about to jump back into the water when his eye caught on something in his field of vision that seemed to rise up from the ground and jut out against the deep navy sky.

It was an enormous rock, half a mile north-west of where he stood, and far enough away to keep Phillips and Davies safe.

Ryan made a split-second decision, and cut back across the moor, throwing himself to the floor when he heard the pop of another bullet being fired. A second later, he was up again, running haphazardly, deliberately changing direction for what seemed like eternity, until he reached what was known locally as the Drake Stone.

He remembered seeing it marked on the map, and knew that it was hard to traverse. But, if he could make it to the top, he knew the angle would be too extreme for his assailant to have a clear shot.

Another bullet popped into the night and flew through the rain to graze the stone by his left shoulder, and Ryan moved quickly around to the other side, hands tracing the wet rockface to find a foothold.

When he did, he heaved himself upward, never more aware that the man he'd seen was lean and fit, and knew the terrain better than he did.

The odds were stacked against him.

Ryan thought of Anna, and of Frank; of Denise and Sam; of Jack and Mel. He thought of his mother and father, and of the sister he'd loved, before she was taken from the world. With every hard step, he thought of them, and of the meaning they brought to his life.

He was not ready to leave them.

* * *

Ryan heard another bullet graze the stone not far from his feet, and fought back the fear that wanted to overpower his body and mind. He gritted his teeth and reached for another foot hold, but the toe of his boot slipped against the rain-slicked stone, and he faltered, his body hanging by his fingertips.

He was near the top now; he knew it, because the man's bullet had been too low, the angle too acute for him to make the shot.

His biceps screamed as he pulled himself up and swung a long leg out to rest it on a high ledge. He knew the man wouldn't be far now, and he heard the sound of running footsteps approaching at speed.

With one last, monumental effort, he dragged himself onto the very top and prepared to wait there, shivering in the darkness.

* * *

"You have to come down eventually."

Ryan knew the man had been circling for a while, like a shark around a lone bather in the sea. He couldn't go down; and the man couldn't come up.

If either of them did, he would die.

They remained in stalemate, the man continuing to circle, while Ryan stayed low in the middle of the flat platform at the very top of the enormous stone. In prehistoric times, Anna had once told him, the druids had used it as a meeting place. In the years following that, it had become known for its supernatural healing powers, and Ryan surprised himself by placing both hands against the rock.

If he had ever needed a stroke of magic, now was the time.

"You'd never have found me, if not by chance," the man was saying now. "I've been living quietly for years, travelling around in my little van, administering relief to those who need it most. You wouldn't understand that."

"I understand you just fine," Ryan replied. "You're not the first person I've met with a hyper-inflated sense of his own importance. That's usually before they hear the clang of the prison door slamming shut behind them."

The man laughed.

"You haven't got the first idea of who you're dealing with," he said, angrily. "I'm not like everyone else."

"What? Because you got yourself a suit made up, you reckon you're a Dark Lord, or something?"

"Shut up. SHUT UP!"

Ryan heard the control in the man's voice beginning to slip away, and wondered if he'd make another stab at trying to clamber up the wall.

He'd almost welcome the fight.

The storm seemed never to end, and he was chilled to the bone, shivering hard as he tried to keep rubbing his arms and legs.

Where were the reinforcements?

But, without a radio, or any other means of contact, how would they know where to look for him?

Ryan kept rubbing his arms and legs to create friction, and hoped it would be enough to last another hour, or however long it would take.

CHAPTER 42

She could hear him, somewhere up ahead.

Beyond the trees, there was a rocky outcrop where one enormous stone rose above them all and looked out across the hills. She could see it, silhouetted against the first light of dawn, and she could hear the man who'd taken refuge at the very top.

Her eyes darted between the stone and the man who continued to circle around it, and knew this was her chance to try to get away, when his attention was focused on somebody else.

The man at the top had looked strong as he raced towards the stone.

He could cope.

But she didn't move, and found herself edging softly forward, using both hands to drag her injured leg along with her. She paused every few seconds, listening, waiting to see if he'd turn around, but he never did.

He was completely distracted.

She felt hate rise up like a tidal wave and her eyes burned with the force of it. She knew that, if she didn't do it, if she didn't face him, she'd be running for the rest of her life.

As she reached the edge of the rocky outcrop, she moved silently, her broken, exhausted body somehow finding the strength to do this one last thing.

One step.

Then another.

Ryan first spotted her at the edge of the trees but knew there was no way to warn her to stay away, or to run for her freedom. She appeared to be injured and, as she stepped closer and closer into the weak light of dawn, he saw she was covered in blood against which he could see the shining whites of her eyes.

Ryan kept the man talking, kept him focused on him as a target—goading him, taunting him as much as he could.

And then, the rain suddenly stopped.

* * *

He heard a slight movement and spun around.

He saw an avenging demon covered in blood and soil, mud and scraps of wool. At that precise moment, there came an enormous flash of lightning which blinded him in the night vision goggles he still wore, so he didn't see the heavy rock come crashing down against his skull.

Ryan heard a sickening *crunch* on the ground below. He took a quick look over the edge and hurried back down the side of the rock, shimmying the last of the distance—but by the time he reached the ground, it was too late.

The woman was kneeling on the floor, bringing the blunt edge of a jagged rock down again and again, though the man was already dead.

"How. Dare. You. Do. This. To. Me!"

Ryan rushed across to catch her hands in his own, taking the weight of the rock and throwing it to one side, where it rolled away.

She was sobbing uncontrollably, her hands covered in his blood and other things, and Ryan took a discreet look at what was left of her captor.

Not much.

"You're safe now," he murmured. "Shh, now. You're safe. I'm with the police. I won't hurt you. You're safe."

He repeated the words until she slumped against his body, and Ryan continued to say soothing words as he lifted her up into his arms and carried her back towards the river, where help awaited them.

EPILOGUE

The soup kitchen was bustling that day, the colder weather having driven more people from the streets and into the little centre where everybody who entered was called a 'friend' and was, more importantly, treated like one. Anna had been volunteering with homeless charities once a week since her student days and, although life could be busy sometimes, she liked to try to keep to her commitment.

As a regular face in the kitchen, Anna had lots of friends there, but it was her surprise visitor that seemed to be causing more of a stir.

"Ooh, pet—can we have a slice of *that* for afters?"

A woman called Doreen, who'd been coming to the kitchen for a year or more, wriggled her eyebrows at the tall, dark stranger who was chopping carrots through the kitchen hatch while he sang along to something on the radio.

"Get away with you, Doreen!" Anna chuckled. "Now, what'll it be? Chicken or vegetable?"

She chatted with everybody who shuffled along the line, until she recognised one she hadn't seen in a couple of weeks.

"David! I was hoping I'd see you today," she said, and began to ladle some chicken soup into a bowl while she chatted. "You know I said I'd have a word with the maintenance team, at the university in Durham? Well, they've got an opening for a maintenance man at Hatfield College. It comes with a little flat, on-site—and the hours seem pretty good. The pay isn't enormous, but it's respectable."

She handed the soldier his bowl, but he struggled to take it all in.

"There's a job, with a flat?"

She nodded.

"They take a small percentage from your salary to pay for household bills, a bit like they do with the students, but otherwise it would be all yours. It would mean moving to Durham…"

Anna paused, wondering if he might not want to. She knew all about David's past history, and about the PTSD he suffered from, so she had tried to find a job that would involve the least stress, whilst allowing him to be useful and provide a valuable service. She wished there were more opportunities available, for all the people in the kitchen, but she knew that David had been searching for a very long time.

"I—thank you. I'd love to do that job."

He thought of quiet walks, at the end of the day—just him and his dog. He could scarcely imagine the thrill of coming home to his own bed at the end of the day, and knowing he'd been the one to earn it.

"That's great. I'll come and see you in a minute, and give you all the contact details."

He nodded, still not quite sure his voice could be trusted.

"Is this your dog?" she asked.

"Yes, this is Naseem," he said proudly.

"You're a very handsome boy," she said, in a voice she hardly recognised as her own. "Would he like some chicken soup?"

Unbelievably, the dog let out a polite *woof,* and she could have sworn that it smiled.

DCI Ryan will return in

Ryan's Christmas: A DCI Ryan Mystery

If you would like to be kept up to date with new releases from LJ Ross, please complete an e-mail contact form on her Facebook page or website, www.ljrossauthor.com

If you enjoy the DCI Ryan Mysteries, why not try
the new series by LJ Ross—
THE ALEXANDER GREGORY THRILLERS?

Read on at the end of this e-book for an exclusive sneak peak at IMPOSTOR—book #1 in the new series—which will be released in all formats on 31st October 2019 and is available for e-book pre-order right now!

AUTHOR'S NOTE

There are lots of themes in here that are very tricky to write about in a way that does justice to the topic, whilst remaining sensitive to those who have been affected by any of the issues involved. Primarily, *Borderlands* is a book about the human condition; it's about relationships between people, and how one small act of kindness can defuse a potentially volatile situation.

It's a very restless world we live in, at the moment, but I wanted to remember all the good that people are trying to do, every day, in their own little ways.

LJ ROSS

September 2019

ACKNOWLEDGMENTS

I've been so lucky during the course of my career—I have, by now, a very long list of people to whom I owe thanks. So many, it would constitute an entirely new book if I were to write them all down! However, I'll limit myself to thanking my lovely husband, James, and my son, Ethan, for being my bedrock; thanks to my gorgeous mum, Susan, and my wonderful dad, Jim, for all their love and support; and to my sister, Rachael, for being generally fabulous! To my friends, I thank you for all your patience while I've been off the radar, buried deep in my writing 'cave', and I'm pleased to be able to tell you I've now crawled out of my office and am available once again for cocktails and dreams, or coffee and cake, as the case may be. Most importantly, my thanks go to you, the Reader, whose kindness means so much to authors like me. We love nothing more than writing stories for people to enjoy and, when that happens, it's the very best of all worlds.

ABOUT THE AUTHOR

LJ Ross is an international bestselling author, best known for creating atmospheric mystery and thriller novels, including the DCI Ryan series of Northumbrian murder mysteries which have sold over four million copies worldwide.

Her debut, *Holy Island*, was released in January 2015 and reached number one in the UK and Australian charts. Since then, she has released a further fourteen novels, all of which have been top three global bestsellers and twelve of which have been UK #1 bestsellers. Louise has garnered an army of loyal readers through her storytelling and, thanks to them, several of her books reached the coveted spot whilst only available to pre-order ahead of release.

Louise was born in Northumberland, England. She studied undergraduate and postgraduate Law at King's College, University of London and then abroad in Paris and Florence. She spent much of her working life in London, where she was a lawyer for a number of years until taking the decision to change career and pursue her dream to write. Now, she writes full time and lives with her husband and son in Northumberland. She enjoys reading all manner of books, travelling and spending time with family and friends.

If you enjoyed *Borderlands*, please consider leaving a review online.

If you would like to be kept up to date with new releases from LJ Ross, please complete an e-mail contact form on her Facebook page or website, www.ljrossauthor.com

IMPOSTOR

AN ALEXANDER GREGORY THRILLER

LJ Ross

PROLOGUE

August 1987

She was muttering again.

The boy heard it from beneath the covers of his bed; an endless, droning sound, like flies swarming a body. The whispering white noise of madness.

Poor, poor baby, she was saying. *My poor, poor baby.*

Over and over she repeated the words, as her feet paced the hallway outside his room. The floorboards creaked as she moved back and forth, until her footsteps came to an abrupt halt.

He hunkered further down, wrapping his arms around his legs, as if the pattern of Jedi knights on his *Star Wars* duvet cover could protect him.

It couldn't.

The door swung open and his mother was silhouetted in its frame, fully dressed despite it being the middle of the night. She strode across the room and shook his coiled body with an unsteady hand.

"Wake up! We need to go to the hospital."

The boy tried not to sigh. She didn't like it when he sighed, when he looked at her the 'wrong' way, or when he argued. Even if he did, she wouldn't listen.

She wouldn't even *hear.*

"I'm awake," he mumbled, although his body was crying out for sleep.

He was always sleepy.

"Come on, get dressed," she continued, and he tried not to look directly at her as she scurried about the room, pulling out clothes at random for him to wear. He didn't want to see her eyes, or what was hidden behind them. They'd be dark again, like they were before, and they'd look straight through him.

There came a soft moan from the bedroom next door, and his mother hurried out, leaving him to pull on jeans and a faded *Power Rangers* t-shirt. The clock on the bedside table told him it was three-seventeen a.m., in cheerful neon-green light. If he had the energy to spare, he might have wondered whether the children he'd seen playing in the garden next door ever got sick, like he did, or whether they got to go to school.

He remembered going to school, once.

He remembered liking it.

But his mother said he was too ill to go to school now, and he'd learn so much more at home, where she could take care of him and Christopher.

It wasn't her fault that, despite all her care, neither boy seemed to get any better.

Once, when she thought he was asleep, she'd come in to sit on the edge of his bed. She'd stroked a hand over his hair and told him that she loved him. For a moment, he thought Mummy had come back; but then, she'd moved her mouth close to his ear and told him it was all because Daddy had left them to be with something called a Filthy Whore, and everything would have been alright if he'd never gone away. He hadn't known what she meant. At first, he'd wondered if some kind of galactic monster had lured his father away. Maybe, at this very moment, he was trapped in a cast of bronze, just like Han Solo.

She called his name, and the boy dragged his skinny body off the bed. There was no time to make up fairy tales about his father, or to wonder how other children lived.

Or how they died.

* * *

There was more muttering at the hospital.

He could hear it, beyond the turquoise curtain surrounding his hospital bed. Whenever somebody passed by, the material rippled on the wind and he caught sight of the serious-looking doctors and nurses gathered a short distance away.

"*I can't see any medical reason—*" he heard one of them say, before the curtain flapped shut again. "*This needs to be reported.*"

"*There have been cases,*" another argued.

"*One dead already, the youngest in critical condition—*"

The boy tensed as he recognised the quick *slap-slap-slap* of his mother's tread against the linoleum floor.

"Where's my son? Where've you taken him?" she demanded, in a shrill voice. "Is he in there?"

He saw her fingers grasp the edge of the curtain, and unconsciously shrank back against the pillows, but she did not pull it back.

There ensued a short argument, conducted in professional undertones.

"If you really think—alright. Yes, yes, he can stay overnight, so long as I stay with him at all times. But what about Christopher?"

The voices receded back down the corridor as they moved towards the High Dependency Unit, where his younger brother lay against scratchy hospital bedsheets, fighting for his life.

* * *

When the boy awoke the next morning, he was not alone.

Three people surrounded his bed. One, he recognised as the doctor who'd snuck him a lollipop the previous night, and she gave him a small smile. Another was a stern-faced man wearing a dark suit that reminded him of his father, and the other was a young woman in a rumpled police uniform with sad brown eyes.

"Hi, there," the doctor said. "How're you doing, champ?"

There was a false note of cheer to her voice that made him nervous.

"W-where's my mum?"

The three adults exchanged an uncomfortable glance.

"You'll see your mother soon," the man told him. "I'm afraid she's had some bad news. You both have."

In careful, neutral tones, they spoke of how his younger brother had died during the night and, with every passing word, the boy's pale, ghostly-white face became more shuttered.

It had happened before, you see.

Last year, his baby sister had died too, before she'd reached her first birthday.

He remembered all the cards and flowers arriving at the house they used to live in; the endless stream of neighbours pouring into his mother's living room to condole and glean a little gossip about their misfortune. He remembered his mother's arm wrapped around his shoulder, cloying and immoveable, like a band of steel.

"*These two are all I have left, now,*" she'd said, tearfully, drawing Christopher tightly against her other side. "*I can only pray that God doesn't take them, too.*"

And, while the mourners tutted and wept and put 'a little something' in envelopes to help out, he'd watched his mother's eyes and wondered why she was so happy.

CHAPTER 1

Ballyfinny

County Mayo, Ireland

Thirty years later

"Daddy, what's an '*eejit*?'"

Liam Kelly exited the roundabout—where he'd recently been cut-up by the aforementioned *eejit* driving a white Range Rover—and rolled his eyes. His three-year-old daughter was growing bigger every day, and apparently her ears were, too.

"That's just a word to describe somebody who…ah, does silly things."

She thought about it.

"Are you an *eejit*, Daddy?"

Liam roared with laughter and smiled in the rear-view mirror.

"It's been said," he admitted, with a wink. "Nearly home now, sugarplum. Shall we tell Mammy all about how well you did in your swimming class, today?"

His daughter grinned and nodded.

"I swam like a fish, didn't I?"

"Aye, you did. Here we are."

It took a minute for him to unbuckle her child seat and to collect their bags, but then Liam and his daughter were skipping hand in hand up the short driveway leading to the front door of their bungalow on the outskirts of the town. It was perched on higher ground overlooking the lough and, though it had been a stretch to buy the place, he was reminded of why they had each time he looked out across the sparkling water.

The front door was open, and they entered the hallway with a clatter of footsteps.

"We're back!" he called out.

But there was not a whisper of sound on the air, and he wondered if his wife was taking a nap. The first trimester was always tiring.

"Maybe Mammy's having a lie-down," he said, and tapped a finger to his lips. "Let's be quiet like mice, alright?"

"Okay," she replied, in a stage whisper.

"You go along and play in your bedroom and I'll bring you a glass of milk in a minute," he said, and smiled as she tiptoed down the corridor with exaggerated care.

When the little girl pushed open the door to her peaches-and-cream bedroom, she didn't notice her mother at first, since she was lying so serenely amongst the stuffed toys on the bed. When she did, she giggled, thinking of the story of Goldilocks.

"You're in my bed!" she whispered.

She crept towards her mother, expecting her eyes to open at any moment.

But they didn't.

The little girl began to feel drowsy after her exertions at the swimming pool, and decided to curl up beside her. She clambered onto the bed and, when her hands brushed her mother's cold skin, she tugged her rainbow blanket over them both.

"That's better," she mumbled, as her eyelids drooped.

When Liam found them lying there a short while later, the glass fell from his nerveless hand and shattered to the floor at his feet. There was a ringing in his ears, the pounding of blood as his body fought to stay upright. He wanted to scream, to shout—to reject the truth of what lay clearly before him.

But there was his daughter to think of.

"C-come here, baby," he managed, even as tears began to fall. "Let's—let's leave Mammy to sleep."

CHAPTER 2

South London

One month later

D octor Alexander Gregory seated himself in one of the easy chairs arranged around a low coffee table in his office, then nodded towards the security liaison nurse who hovered in the doorway.

"I'll take it from here, Pete."

The man glanced briefly at the other occupant in the room, then stepped outside to station himself within range, should his help be required.

After the door clicked shut, Gregory turned his attention to the woman seated opposite. Cathy Jones was in her early sixties but looked much younger; as though life's cares had taken very little toll. Her hair was dyed and cut into a snazzy style by a mobile hairdresser who visited the hospital every few weeks. She wore jeans and a cream wool jumper, but no jewellery—as per the rules. Her fingernails were painted a daring shade of purple and she had taken time with her make-up, which was flawless. For all the world, she could have been one of the smart, middle-aged women he saw sipping rosé at a wine bar in the city, dipping focaccia bread into small bowls of olive oil and balsamic while they chatted with their friends about the latest episode of *Strictly Come Dancing*.

That is, if she hadn't spent much of the past thirty years detained under the Mental Health Act.

"It's nice to see you again, Cathy. How was your week?"

They went through a similar dance every Thursday afternoon, where he asked a series of gentle, social questions to put her at ease, before attempting to delve into the deeper ones in accordance with her care plan. Though he was generally optimistic by nature, Gregory did not hold out any great hope that, after so long in the system, the most recent strategy of individual and group sessions, art and music therapy, would bring this woman any closer to re-entering normal society—but he had to try.

Cathy leaned forward suddenly, her eyes imploring him to listen.

"I wanted to speak to you, Doctor," she said, urgently. "It's about the next review meeting."

"Your care plan was reviewed recently," he said, in an even tone. "Don't you remember?"

There was a flicker of frustration, quickly masked.

"The clinical team made a mistake," she said.

"Oh? What might that be?"

Gregory crossed one leg lightly over the other and reached for his notepad, ready to jot down the latest theory she had cobbled together to explain the reason for her being there in the first place. In thirty years as a patient in four different secure hospitals, under the care of numerous healthcare professionals, Cathy had never accepted the diagnosis of her condition.

Consequently, she hadn't shown a scrap of remorse for her crimes, either.

"Well, I was reading only the other day about that poor, *poor* mother whose baby died. You know the one?"

Gregory did. The tragic case of Sudden Infant Death Syndrome had been widely reported in the press, but he had no intention of sating this woman's lust for tales of sensational child-deaths.

"Anyway, all those years ago, when they put me in *here*, the doctors didn't know so much about cot death. Not as much as they do now. If they had, things might have been different—"

Gregory looked up from his notepad, unwilling to entertain the fantasies that fed her illness.

"Do you remember the reason the pathologist gave for the deaths of your daughter, Emily, and your son, Christopher? Neither of them died following Sudden Infant Death Syndrome, as I think you're well aware."

The room fell silent, and she stared at him with mounting hatred, which he studiously ignored. Somewhere behind the reinforced glass window, they heard the distant buzz of a security gate opening.

"It was a cover up," she said, eventually. "You doctors are all the same. You always cover for each other. My children were *ill*, and not one of those quacks knew what to do about it—"

Gregory weighed up the usefulness of fishing out the pathology reports completed in 1987 following the murders of a two-year-old boy and a girl of nine months.

Not today.

"I'm going to appeal the court ruling," she declared, though every one of her previous attempts had failed. "You know what your problem is, Doctor? You've spent so long working with crackpots, you can't tell when a sane person comes along."

She'd tried this before, too. It was a favourite pastime of hers, to try to beat the doctor at his own game. It was a classic symptom of Munchausen's that the sufferer developed an obsessive interest in the medical world, and its terminology. Usually, in order to find the best way to disguise the fact they were slowly, but surely, killing their own children.

"How did it make you feel, when your husband left you, Cathy?"

Gregory nipped any forthcoming tirade neatly in the bud, and she was momentarily disarmed. Then, she gave an ugly laugh.

"Back to that old chestnut again, are we?"

When he made no reply, she ran an agitated hand through her hair.

"How would any woman feel?" she burst out. "He left me with three children, for some *tart* with cotton wool for brains. I was well rid of him."

But her index finger began to tap against the side of the chair.

Tap, tap, tap.

Tap, tap, tap.

"When was the divorce finalised, Cathy?"

"It's all there in your bloody file, isn't it?" she spat. "Why bother to ask?"

"I'm interested to know if you remember."

"Sometime in 1985," she muttered. "January, February…Emily was only a couple of months old. The bastard was at it the whole time I was pregnant."

"That must have been very hard. Why don't you tell me about it?"

Her eyes skittered about the room, all of her previous composure having evaporated.

"There's nothing to tell. He buggered off to Geneva to live in a bloody great mansion with his Barbie doll, while I was left to bring up his children. He barely even called when Emily was rushed into hospital. When *any* of them were."

"Do you think their…*illness*, would have improved, if he had?"

She gave him a sly look.

"How could it have made a difference? They were suffering from very rare conditions, outside our control."

Gregory's lips twisted, but he tried again.

"Did a part of you hope that news of their 'illness' might have encouraged your husband to return to the family home?"

"I never thought of it," she said. "All of my thoughts and prayers were spent trying to save my children."

He glanced up at the large, white plastic clock hanging on the wall above her head.

It was going to be a long morning.

* * *

An hour after Gregory finished his session with Cathy, he had just finished typing up his notes when a loud siren began to wail.

He threw open the door to his office and ran into the corridor, where the emergency alarm was louder still, echoing around the walls in a cacophony of sound. He took a quick glance in both directions and spotted a red flashing light above the doorway of one of the patients' rooms. He sprinted towards it, dimly aware of running footsteps following his own as others responded to whatever awaited them beyond the garish red light.

The heels of his shoes skidded against the floor as he reached the open doorway, where he found one of the ward nurses engaged in a mental battle with a patient who had fashioned a rudimentary knife from a sharpened fragment of metal and was presently holding it against her own neck.

Gregory reached for the alarm button and, a moment later, the wailing stopped. In the residual silence, he took a deep breath and fell back on his training.

"Do you mind if I come in?" he asked, holding out his hands, palms outstretched in the universal gesture for peace.

He exchanged a glance with the nurse, who was holding up well. He'd never ascribed to old-school hierarchies within hospital walls; doctors were no better equipped to deal with situations of this kind than an experienced mental health nurse—in fact, the reverse was often true. Life at Southmoor High Security Psychiatric Hospital followed a strict routine, for very good reason. Depending on their level of risk, patients were checked at least every fifteen minutes to try to prevent suicide attempts being made, even by those who had shown no inclination before, or who had previously been judged 'low risk'.

Especially those.

There were few certainties in the field of mental healthcare, but uncertainty was one of them.

"I'd like you to put the weapon down, Hannah," he said, calmly. "It's almost lunchtime, and it's Thursday. You know what that means."

As he'd hoped, she looked up, her grip on the knife loosening a fraction.

"Jam roly-poly day," he smiled. It was a mutual favourite of theirs and, in times of crisis, he needed to find common ground.

Anything to keep her alive.

"Sorry, Doc," she whispered, and plunged the knife into her throat…

IMPOSTOR will be released in all formats on 31st October 2019 and is available for e-book pre-order now!

30816278R10147

Printed in Great
Britain
by Amazon